VINTAGE

INTERNATIONAL

The
Passion

ALSO BY JEANETTE WINTERSON

Oranges Are Not the Only Fruit

The
Passion

Jeanette Winterson

VINTAGE INTERNATIONAL

Vintage Books
A Division of Random House, Inc.
New York

First Vintage International Edition, October 1989

Library of Congress Cataloging-in-Publication Data
Winterson, Jeanette, 1959–
    The passion / Jeanette Winterson.—1st Vintage international ed.
        p.   cm.—(Vintage international)
    ISBN 0-679-72437-0
    I. Title.
[PR6073.I558P36   1989]
823'.914—dc20   89-40146
                                                                              CIP

Display typography by Rebecca Aidlin

Manufactured in the United States of America
79B8

For Pat Kavanagh

My thanks are due to Don and Ruth Rendell whose hospitality gave me the space to work. To everyone at Bloomsbury, especially Liz Calder. To Philippa Brewster for her patience.

You have navigated with raging soul far from the <u>paternal</u> home, passing beyond the seas' double rocks and now you inhabit a foreign land.

Medea

Contents

1   The Emperor   1
2   The Queen of Spades   47
3   The Zero Winter   77
4   The Rock   131

· 1 ·

the Emperor

It was Napoleon who had such a passion for chicken that he kept his chefs working around the clock. What a kitchen that was, with birds in every state of undress; some still cold and slung over hooks, some turning slowly on the spit, but most in wasted piles because the Emperor was busy.

Odd to be so governed by an appetite.

It was my first commission. I started as a neck wringer and before long I was the one who carried the platter through inches of mud to his tent. He liked me because I am short. I flatter myself. He did not dislike me. He liked no one except Joséphine and he liked her the way he liked chicken.

No one over five foot two ever waited on the Emperor. He kept small servants and large horses. The horse he loved was seventeen hands high with a tail that could wrap round a man three times and still make a wig for his mistress. That horse had the evil eye and there's been almost as many dead grooms in the stable as chickens on the table. The ones the beast didn't kill itself with an easy kick, its master had disposed of because its coat didn't shine or the bit was green.

'A new government must dazzle and amaze,' he said. Bread and circuses I think he said. Not surprising then that when we did find a groom, he came from a circus himself and stood as high as the horse's flank. When he brushed the beast he used a ladder with a stout bottom and a triangle top, but when he rode him for exercise he took a great leap and landed square on the glossy back while the horse reared and snorted and couldn't throw him, not even with its nose in the dirt and its back legs towards God. Then they'd vanish in a curtain of dust and travel for miles, the midget clinging to the mane and whooping in his funny language that none of us could understand.

But he understood everything.

He made the Emperor laugh and the horse couldn't better him, so he stayed. And I stayed. And we became friends.

We were in the kitchen tent one night when the bell starts ringing like the Devil himself is on the other end. We all jumped up and one rushed to the spit while another spat on the silver and I had to get my boots back on ready for that tramp across the frozen ruts. The midget laughed and said he'd rather take a chance with the horse than the master, but we don't laugh.

Here it comes surrounded by parsley the cook cherishes in a dead man's helmet. Outside the flakes are so dense that I feel like the little figure in a child's snowstorm. I have to screw up my eyes to follow the yellow stain that lights up Napoleon's tent. No one else can have a light at this time of night.

Fuel's scarce. Not all of this army have tents.

When I go in, he's sitting alone with a globe in front of him. He doesn't notice me, he goes on turning the globe round and round, holding it tenderly with both hands as if it were a breast. I give a short cough and he looks up suddenly with fear in his face.

'Put it here and go.'

'Don't you want me to carve it, Sir?'

'I can manage. Goodnight.'

I know what he means. He hardly ever asks me to carve now. As soon as I'm gone he'll lift the lid and pick it up and push it into his mouth. He wishes his whole face were mouth to cram a whole bird.

In the morning I'll be lucky to find the wishbone.

There is no heat, only degrees of cold. I don't remember the feeling of a fire against my knees. Even in the kitchen, the warmest place on any camp, the heat is too thin to spread and the copper pans cloud over. I take off my socks once a week to cut my toe-nails and the others call me a dandy. We're white with red noses and blue fingers.

The tricolour.

He does it to keep his chickens fresh.

He uses winter like a larder.

But that was a long time ago. In Russia.

Nowadays people talk about the things he did as though they made sense. As though even his most disastrous mistakes were only the result of bad luck or hubris.

It was a mess.

Words like devastation, rape, slaughter, carnage, starvation are lock and key words to keep the pain at bay. Words about war that are easy on the eye.

I'm telling you stories. Trust me.

I wanted to be a drummer.

The recruiting officer gave me a walnut and asked if I could crack it between finger and thumb. I could not and he laughed and said a drummer must have strong hands. I stretched out my palm, the walnut resting there, and offered him the same challenge. He coloured up and had a Lieutenant take me to the kitchen tents. The cook sized up my skinny frame and reckoned I was not a cleaver man. Not for me the mess of unnamed meat that had to be chopped for the daily stew. He said I was lucky, that I would be working for Bonaparte himself, and for one brief, bright moment I imagined a training as a pastry cook building delicate towers of sugar and cream. We walked towards a small tent with two impassive guards by the flaps.

'Bonaparte's own storeroom,' said the cook.

The space from the ground to the dome of the canvas was racked with rough wooden cages about a foot square with tiny corridors running in between, hardly the width of a man. In each cage there were two or three birds, beaks and claws cut off, staring through the slats with dumb identical eyes. I am no coward and I've seen plenty of convenient mutilation on our farms but I was not prepared for the silence. Not even a rustle. They could have been dead, should have been dead, but for the eyes. The cook turned to go. 'Your job is to clear them out and wring their necks.'

I slipped away to the docks, and because the stone was warm in that early April and because I had been travelling for days I fell asleep dreaming of drums and a red uniform. It was a boot that woke me, hard and shiny with a familiar saddle smell. I raised my head and saw it resting on my belly the way I had rested the walnut in my palm. The officer didn't look at me, but said, 'You're a soldier now and you'll get plenty of opportunity to sleep in the open air. On your feet.'

He lifted his foot and, as I scrambled up, kicked me hard and still looking straight ahead said, 'Firm buttocks, that's something.'

I heard of his reputation soon enough but he never bothered me. I think the chicken smell kept him away.

I was homesick from the start. I missed my mother. I missed the hill where the sun slants across the valley. I missed all the everyday things I had hated. In spring at home the dandelions streak the fields and the river runs idle again after months of rain. When the army recruitment came it was a brave band of us who laughed and said it was time we saw more than the red barn and the cows we had birthed. We signed up straight away and those of us who couldn't write made an optimistic smear on the page.

Our village holds a bonfire every year at the end of winter. We had been building it for weeks, tall as a cathedral with a blasphemous spire of broken snares and infested pallets. There would be plenty of wine and dancing and a sweetheart in the dark and because we were leaving we were allowed to light it. As the sun went down we plunged our five burning brands into the heart of the pyre. My mouth went dry as I heard the wood take and splinter until the first flame pushed its way out. I wished I were a holy man then with an angel to protect me so I could jump inside the fire and see my sins burned away. I go to confession but there's no fervour there. Do it from the heart or not at all.

We're a lukewarm people for all our feast days and hard work. Not much touches us, but we long to be touched. We lie awake at night willing the darkness to part and show us a vision. Our children frighten us in their intimacy, but we make sure they grow up like us. Lukewarm like us. On a night like this, hands and faces hot, we can believe that tomorrow will show us angels in jars and that the well-known woods will suddenly reveal another path.

Last time we had this bonfire, a neighbour tried to pull down the boards of his house. He said it was nothing but a stinking pile of dung, dried meat and lice. He said he was going to burn the lot. His wife was tugging at his arms. She was a big woman, used to the churn and the field, but she couldn't stop him. He smashed his fist into the seasoned wood until his hand looked like a skinned lamb's head. Then he lay by the fire all night until the early wind covered him in cooling ash. He never spoke of it. We never spoke of it. He doesn't come to the bonfire any more.

I sometimes wonder why none of us tried to stop him. I think we wanted him to do it, to do it for us. To tear down our long-houred lives and let us start again. Clean and simple with open hands. It wouldn't be like that, no more than it could have been like that when Bonaparte set fire to half of Europe.

But what other chance had we?

Morning came and we marched away with our parcels of bread and ripe cheese. There were tears from the women and the men slapped us on the back and said soldiering is a fine life for a boy. One little girl who always followed me around pulled at my hand, her eyebrows close together with worry.

'Will you kill people, Henri?'

I dropped down beside her. 'Not people, Louise, just the enemy.'

'What is enemy?'

'Someone who's not on your side.'

We were on our way to join the Army of England at Boulogne. Boulogne, a sleepy nothing port with a handful of whorehouses, suddenly became the springboard of Empire. Only twenty miles away, easy to see on a clear day, was England and her arrogance. We knew about the English; how they ate their children and ignored the Blessed Virgin. How they committed suicide with unseemly cheerfulness. The English have the highest suicide rate in Europe. I got that straight from a priest. The English with their John Bull beef and frothing beer. The English who are even now waist-high in the waters off Kent practising to drown the best army in the world.

We are to invade England.

All France will be recruited if necessary. Bonaparte will snatch up his country like a sponge and wring out every last drop.

We are in love with him.

At Boulogne, though my hopes of drumming head high at the front of a proud column are dashed, I'm still head high enough because I know I'll see Bonaparte himself. He comes regularly rattling from the Tuileries and scanning the seas like an ordinary man checks his rain barrel. Domino the midget says that being near him is like having a great wind rush about your ears. He says that's how Madame de Staël put it and she's famous enough to be right. She doesn't live in France now. Bonaparte had her exiled because she complained about him censoring the theatre and suppressing the newspapers. I once bought a book of hers from a travelling pedlar who'd had it from a ragged nobleman. I didn't understand much but I learned the word 'intellectual' which I would like to apply to myself.

Domino laughs at me.

At night I dream of dandelions.

The cook grabbed a chicken from the hook above his head and scooped a handful of stuffing from the copper bowl.

He was smiling.

'Out on the town tonight, lads, and a night to remember, I swear it.' He rammed the stuffing inside the bird, twisting his hand to get an even coating.

'You've all had a woman before I suppose?'

Most of us blushed and some of us giggled.

'If you haven't then there's nothing sweeter and if you have, well, Bonaparte himself doesn't tire of the same taste day after day.'

He held up the chicken for our inspection.

I had hoped to stay in with the pocket Bible given to me by my mother as I left. My mother loved God, she said that God and the Virgin were all she needed though she was thankful for her family. I've seen her kneeling before dawn, before the milking, before the thick porridge, and singing out loud to God, whom she has never seen. We're more or less religious in our village and we honour the priest who tramps seven miles to bring us the wafer, but it doesn't pierce our hearts.

St Paul said it is better to marry than to burn, but my mother taught me it is better to burn than to marry. She wanted to be a nun. She hoped I would be a priest and saved to give me an education while my friends plaited rope and trailed after the plough.

I can't be a priest because although my heart is as loud as hers I can pretend no answering riot. I have shouted to God and the Virgin, but they have not shouted back and I'm not interested in the still small voice. Surely a god can meet passion with passion?

She says he can.

Then he should.

My mother's family were not wealthy but they were respectable. She was brought up quietly on music and suitable literature, and politics were never discussed at table, even when the rebels were breaking down the doors. Her family were monarchists. When she was twelve she told them that she wanted to be a nun, but they disliked excess and assured her that marriage would be more fulfilling. She grew in secret, away from their eyes. Outwardly she was obedient and loving, but inside she was feeding a hunger that would have disgusted them if disgust itself were not an excess. She read the lives of saints and knew most of the Bible off by heart. She believed that the Blessed Virgin herself would aid her when the time came.

The time came when she was fifteen, at a cattle fair. Most of the town was out to see the lumbering bullocks and high-pitched sheep. Her mother and father were in holiday mood and in a rash moment her papa pointed to a stout, well-dressed man carrying a child on his shoulders. He said she couldn't do better for a husband. He would be dining with them later and very much hoped that Georgette (my mother) would sing after supper. When the crowd thickened my mother made her escape, taking nothing with her but the clothes she stood in and her Bible that she always carried. She hid in a haycart and set off that sunburnt evening out of the town and slowly through the quiet country until the cart reached the village of my birth. Quite without fear, because she believed in the power of the Virgin, my mother presented herself to Claude (my father) and asked to be taken to the nearest convent. He was a slow-witted but kindly man, ten years older than her, and he offered her a bed for the night, thinking to take her home the next day and maybe collect a reward.

She never went home and she never found the convent either. The days turned into weeks and she was afraid of her father, who she heard was scouring the area and leaving bribes at any religious houses he passed. Three months went by and she discovered that she had a way with plants and that she could quiet frightened animals. Claude hardly ever spoke to her and never bothered her, but sometimes she would catch him watching her, standing still with his hand shading his eyes.

One night, late, as she slept, she heard a tapping at the door and turning up her lamp saw Claude in the doorway. He had shaved, he was wearing his nightshirt and he smelled of carbolic soap.

'Will you marry me, Georgette?'

She shook her head and he went away, returning now and again as time continued, always standing by the door, clean shaven and smelling of soap.

She said yes. She couldn't go home. She couldn't go to a convent so long as her father was bribing every Mother Superior with a mind to a new altar piece, but she couldn't go on living with this quiet man and his talkative neighbours unless he married her. He got into bed beside her and stroked her face and taking her hand put it to his face. She was not afraid. She believed in the power of the Virgin.

After that, whenever he wanted her, he tapped at the door in just the same way and waited until she said yes.

Then I was born.

She told me about my grandparents and their house and their piano, and a shadow crossed her eyes when she thought I would never see them, but I liked my anonymity. Everyone else in the village had strings of relations to pick fights with and know about. I made up stories about mine. They were whatever I wanted them to be depending on my mood.

Thanks to my mother's efforts and the rusty scholarliness of our priest I learned to read in my own language, Latin and English and I learned arithmetic, the rudiments of first aid and because the priest also supplemented his meagre income by betting and gambling I learned every card game and a few tricks. I never told my mother that the priest had a hollow Bible with a pack of cards inside. Sometimes he took it to our service by mistake and then the reading was always from the first chapter of Genesis. The villagers thought he loved the creation story. He was a good man but lukewarm. I would have preferred a burning Jesuit, perhaps then I might have found the extasy I need to believe.

I asked him why he was a priest, and he said if you have to work for anybody an absentee boss is best.

We fished together and he pointed out the girls he wanted and asked me to do it for him. I never did. I came to women late like my father.

When I left, Mother didn't cry. It was Claude who cried. She gave me her little Bible, the one that she had kept for so many years, and I promised her I would read it.

The cook saw my hesitation and poked me with a skewer. 'New to it, lad? Don't be afraid. These girls I know are clean as a whistle and wide as the fields of France.' I got ready, washing myself all over with carbolic soap.

Bonaparte, the Corsican. Born in 1769, a Leo.

Short, pale, moody, with an eye to the future and a singular ability to concentrate. In 1789 revolution opened a closed world and for a time the meanest street boy had more on his side than any aristocrat. For a young Lieutenant skilled in artillery, the chances were kind and in a few years General Bonaparte was turning Italy into the fields of France.

'What is luck', he said, 'but the ability to exploit accidents?' He believed he was the centre of the world and for a long time there was nothing to change him from this belief. Not even John Bull. He was in love with himself and France joined in. It was a romance. Perhaps all romance is like that; not a contract between equal parties but an explosion of dreams and desires that can find no outlet in everyday life. Only a drama will do and while the fireworks last the sky is a different colour. He became an Emperor. He called the Pope from the Holy City to crown him but at the last second he took the crown in his own hands and placed it on his own head. He divorced the only person who understood him, the only person he ever really loved, because she couldn't give him a child. That was the only part of the romance he couldn't manage by himself.

He is repulsive and fascinating by turns.

What would you do if you were an Emperor? Would soldiers become numbers? Would battles become diagrams? Would intellectuals become a threat? Would you end your days on an island where the food is salty and the company bland?

He was the most powerful man in the world and he couldn't beat Joséphine at billiards.

I'm telling you stories. Trust me.

The brothel was run by a giantess from Sweden. Her hair was yellow like dandelions and like a living rug it covered her knees. Her arms were bare, the dress she wore had the sleeves pushed up and fastened with a pair of garters. Around her neck on a leather thong she kept a flat-faced wooden doll. She saw me staring at it and drawing my head close forced me to sniff it. It smelled of musk and strange flowers.

'From Martinique, like Bonaparte's Joséphine.'

I smiled and said, 'Vive notre dame de victoires,' but the giantess laughed and said that Joséphine would never be crowned

in Westminster as Bonaparte had promised. The cook told her
sharply to mind her words, but she had no fear of him and led
us to a cold stone room furnished with pallet beds and a long
table stacked with jars of red wine. I had expected red velvet the
way the priest had described these seats of temporary pleasure,
but there was no softness here, nothing to disguise our business.
When the women came in they were older than I had imagined,
not at all like the pictures in the priest's book of sinful things.
Not snake-like, Eve-like with breasts like apples, but round and
resigned, hair thrown into hasty bundles or draped around their
shoulders. My companions brayed and whistled and shoved the
wine down their throats straight from the jars. I wanted a cup
of water but didn't know how to ask.

The cook moved first, slapping a woman on the rump and
making some joke about her corset. He still wore his fat-stained
boots. The others started to pair off leaving me with a patient
black-toothed woman who had ten rings on one finger.

'I've just joined up,' I told her, hoping she'd realise that I
didn't know what to do.

She pinched my cheek. 'That's what they all say, they think it
must be cheaper first time. Hard work I call it, like teaching
billiards without a cue.' She looked over at the cook, who was
squatting on one of the pallets trying to get his cock out. His
woman knelt in front of him, her arms folded. Suddenly he slapped her across the face and the snap killed the talk for a moment.

'Help me, you bitch, put your hand in, can't you, or are you
afraid of eels?'

I saw her lip curl and the red mark on her cheek glowed
despite her rough skin. She didn't answer, just poked her hand
into his trousers and brought it out like a ferret by the neck.

'In your mouth.'

I was thinking about porridge.

'Fine man your friend,' said my woman.

I wanted to go to him and ram his face in the blanket until

he had no breath left. Then he came with a great bellow and flopped backwards on his elbows. His woman got up and very deliberately spat in the bowl on the floor, then rinsed her mouth with wine and spat that out too. She was noisy and the cook heard and asked her what she was doing throwing his sperm to the sewers of France.

'What else would I do with it?'

He came towards her with his fist raised but it never fell. My woman stepped forward and coshed him on the back of the head with a wine jar. She held her companion for a moment and kissed her swiftly on the forehead.

She would never do that to me.

I told her I had a headache and went to sit outside.

We carried our leader home taking turns in fours to bear him like a coffin on our shoulders, face down in case he vomited. In the morning he swaggered over to the officers and boasted how he'd made the bitch swallow him whole and how her cheeks had filled out like a rat's when she took him.

'What happened to your head?'

'Fell over on the way back,' he said, looking at me.

He went out whoring most nights but I never went with him again. Apart from Domino and Patrick, the de-frocked priest with the eagle eye, I hardly spoke to anyone. I spent my time learning how to stuff a chicken and slow down the cooking process. I was waiting for Bonaparte.

At last, on a hot morning when the sea left salt craters in between the dock stones, he came. He came with his Generals Murat and Bernadotte. He came with his new Admiral of the Fleet. He came with his wife, whose grace made the roughest in the camp polish his boots twice. But I saw no one but him. For years, my mentor, the priest who had supported the Revolution, told me that Bonaparte was perhaps the Son of God come again. I learned his battles and campaigns instead of history and geography. I have lain with the priest on an old and impossibly folded map of the world looking at the places he had gone and watching the frontiers of France push slowly out. The priest carried a drawing of Bonaparte next to his drawing of the Blessed Virgin and I grew up with both, unknown to my mother, who remained a monarchist and who still prayed for the soul of Marie Antoinette.

I was only five when the Revolution turned Paris into a free man's city and France into the scourge of Europe. Our village was not very far down the Seine, but we might have been living on the moon. No one really knew what was happening except that King and Queen were imprisoned. We relied on gossip, but the priest crept back and forth relying on his cloth to save him from the cannon or the knife. The village was divided. Most felt King and Queen are right though King and Queen had no care for us, except as revenue and scenery. But these are my words, taught to me by a clever man who was no respecter of persons. For the most part, my friends in the village could not speak of their unease, but I saw it in their shoulders as they rounded up the cattle, saw it in their faces as they listened to the priest in church. We were always helpless, whoever was in power.

The priest said we were living in the last days, that the Revolution would bring forth a new Messiah and the millennium on earth. He never went as far as that in church. He told me. Not the others. Not Claude with his pails, not Jacques in the dark with his sweetheart, not my mother with her prayers. He took me on his knees, holding me against the black cloth that smelled of age and hay, and told me not to be afraid of rumours in our village that everyone in Paris was either starving or dead. 'Christ said he came not to bring peace but a sword, Henri, remember that.'

As I grew older and the turbulent times settled into something like calm, Bonaparte began to make a name for himself. We called him our Emperor long before he had taken that title to himself. And on our way home from the makeshift church in the dusk in winter, the priest looked towards the track that led away and held my arm too tight. 'He'll call you,' he whispered, 'like God called Samuel and you'll go.'

We were not training on the day he came. He caught us out, probably on purpose, and when the first exhausted messenger galloped into the camp warning us that Bonaparte was travelling non-stop and would arrive before noon we were sprawled in our shirt-sleeves drinking coffee and playing dice. The officers were wild with fear and began organising their men as though the English themselves had landed. There was no reception prepared for him, his specially designed bivouac housed a pair of cannon and the cook was blind drunk.

'You.' I was seized by a Captain I did not recognise. 'Do something about the birds. Never mind your uniform, you'll be busy while we're on parade.'

So this was it, no glory for me, just a pile of dead birds.

In my rage I filled up the largest fish-kettle I could and poured cold water all over the cook. He didn't stir.

An hour later, when the birds were staggered on the spits to cook in their turn, the Captain came back very agitated and told me that Bonaparte wanted to inspect the kitchens. It was always a feature of his to interest himself in every detail of his army, but this was inconvenient.

'Get that man out of here,' ordered the Captain as he left. The cook weighed around 200 lbs, I was scarcely 120. I tried raising his upper body and dragging him, but I could only manage a helpless shuffle.

If I had been a prophet and this cook the heathen agent of a false god I could have prayed to the Lord and had a host of angels move him. As it was, Domino came to my aid with some talk about Egypt.

I knew about Egypt because Bonaparte had been there. His Egyptian campaign, doomed but brave, where he had remained immune from the plague and the fever and ridden miles in the dust without a drop of water.

'How could he,' the priest had said, 'if he isn't protected by God?'

It was Domino's plan to raise the cook the way the Egyptians raised their obelisks, with a fulcrum, in our case an oar. We levered the oar under his back, then dug a pit at his feet.

'Now,' said Domino. 'All our weight on the end of the oar and he'll go up.'

It was Lazarus being raised from the dead.

We got him standing and I wedged the oar beneath his belt to stop him falling over.

'What do we do now, Domino?'

While we stood on either side of this mound of flesh, the tent flap parted and the Captain strode in, very proper. Colour drained from his face as though someone had pulled a plug in his throat. He opened his mouth and his moustache moved but that was all.

Pushing past him was Bonaparte.

He walked twice round our exhibit and asked who he was.

'The cook, Sir. A little bit drunk, Sir. These men were removing him.'

I was desperate to get to the spit where one of the chickens was already burning, but Domino stepped in front of me and, speaking in a rough language he later told me was Bonaparte's Corsican dialect, he somehow explained what had happened and how we had done our best on the lines of his Egyptian campaign. When Domino had done, Bonaparte came towards me and pinched my ear so that it was swollen for days.

'You see, Captain,' he said, 'this is what makes my army invincible, the ingenuity and determination of even the humblest soldier.' The Captain smiled weakly, then Bonaparte turned to me. 'You'll see great things and you'll eat your dinner off an

Englishman's plate before long. Captain, see to it that this boy waits on me personally. There will be no weak links in my army, I want my attendants to be as reliable as my Generals. Domino, we are riding this afternoon.'

I wrote to my friend the priest straight away. This was more perfect than any ordinary miracle. I had been chosen. I didn't foresee that the cook would become my sworn enemy. By nightfall most of the camp had heard the story and had embroidered it, so that we had buried the cook in a trench, beaten him unconscious, or most bizarre of all, that Domino had worked a spell on him.

'If only I knew how,' he said. 'We could have saved ourselves the digging.'

The cook, who sobered up with a thumping head and in a worse temper than usual, couldn't step outside without some soldier winking and poking at him. Finally he came to where I sat with my little Bible and grabbed me close by the collar.

'You think you're safe because Bonaparte wants you. You're safe now, but there are years ahead.'

He pushed me back against the onion sacks and spat in my face. It was a long time before we met again because the Captain had him transferred to the stores outside Boulogne.

'Forget him,' said Domino when we watched him leave on the back of a cart.

It's hard to remember that this day will never come again. That the time is now and the place is here and that there are no second chances at a single moment. During the days that Bonaparte stayed in Boulogne there was a feeling of urgency and privilege. He woke before us and slept long after us, going through every detail of our training and rallying us personally. He stretched his hand towards the Channel and made England sound as though she already belonged to us. To each of us. That was his gift. He became the focus of our lives. The thought of fighting excited us. No one wants to be killed but the hardship, the long hours, the cold, the orders were things we would have endured anyway on the farms or in the towns. We were not free men. He made sense out of dullness.

The ridiculous flat-bottomed barges built in their hundreds took on the certainty of galleons. When we put out to sea, practising for that treacherous twenty-mile crossing, we no longer made jokes about shrimping nets or how these tubs would better serve washerwomen. While he stood on the shore shouting orders we put our faces to the wind and let our hearts go out to him.

The barges were designed to carry sixty men and it was reckoned that 20,000 of us would be lost on the way over or picked off by the English before we landed. Bonaparte thought them good odds, he was used to losing that number in battle. None of us worried about being one of the 20,000. We hadn't joined up to worry.

According to his plan, if the French navy could hold the Channel for just six hours, he could land his army and England would be his. It seemed absurdly easy. Nelson himself couldn't outwit us in six hours. We laughed at the English and most of us had plans for our visit there. I particularly wanted to visit the Tower of London because the priest had told me it was full of orphans; bastards of aristocratic descent whose parents were too ashamed to keep them at home. We're not like that in France, we welcome our children.

Domino told me that we were rumoured to be digging a tunnel ready to pop up like moles in the Kentish fields. 'It took us an hour to dig a foot pit for your friend.'

Other stories concerned a balloon landing, a man-firing cannon and a plan to blow up the Houses of Parliament just as Guy Fawkes had nearly done. The balloon landing was the one the English were taking the most seriously and, to prevent us, they built tall towers along the Cinque Ports, to spot us and to shoot us down.

All folly, but I think if Bonaparte had asked us to strap on wings and fly to St James's Palace we would have set off as confidently as a child lets loose a kite.

Without him, during nights and days when affairs of state took him back to Paris, our nights and days were different only in the amount of light they let in. For myself, with no one to love, a hedgehog spirit seemed best and I hid my heart in the leaves.

I have a way with priests, so it came as no surprise that along with Domino, my friend should be Patrick, the de-frocked priest with the eagle eye, imported from Ireland.

In 1799, when Napoleon was still vying for power, General Hoche, a schoolboys' hero and onetime lover of Madame Bonaparte, had landed in Ireland and almost succeeded in defeating John Bull outright. During his stay he heard a story about a certain disgraced priest whose right eye was just like yours or mine, but whose left eye could put the best telescope to shame. Indeed he had been forced out of the church for squinting at young girls from the bell tower. What priest doesn't? But in Patrick's case, thanks to the miraculous properties of his eye, no bosom was safe. A girl might be undressing two villages away, but if the evening was clear and her shutters were back she might just as well have gone to the priest and lain her underclothes at his feet.

Hoche, a man of the world, was sceptical of old wives' tales, but soon found that the women were wiser than he. Though Patrick at first denied the charge and the men laughed and said women and their fantasies, the women looked at the earth and said they knew when they were being watched. The Bishop had taken them seriously, not because he believed the talk about Patrick's eye, but preferring the smooth shapes of his choirboys he found the affair exceedingly repulsive.

A priest should have better things to do than look at women. Hoche, caught in this web of hearsay, took Patrick drinking till the man could hardly stand, then half-walked, half-carried him to a hillock that afforded a clear view across the valley for some miles. They sat together and, while Patrick dozed, Hoche pulled out a red flag and waved it for a couple of minutes. Then nudging Patrick awake he commented, as one would, on the splendid evening and the beautiful scenery. Out of courtesy to his host Patrick forced himself to follow the sweep of Hoche's arm, muttering something about the Irish having been blessed with their portion of paradise on earth. Then he propped himself forward, screwed up one eye, and in a voice as hushed and holy as the Bishop's at communion said, 'Would you look at that now?'

'At what, that falcon?'

'Never mind the falcon, she's as strong and brown as a cow.' Hoche could see nothing, but he knew what Patrick could see. He had paid a tart to undress in a field some fifteen miles away, and placed his men at regular intervals with their red flags.

When he left for France he took Patrick with him.

At Boulogne, Patrick was usually to be found, like Simeon Stylites, on the top of a purpose-built pillar. From there he could look out across the Channel and report on the whereabouts of Nelson's blockading fleet and warn our practising troops of any English threat. French boats that strayed too far out of the harbour radius were likely to be picked off with a sharp broadside if the English were in the mood for patrolling. In order to alert us, Patrick had been given an Alpine horn as tall as a man. On foggy nights this melancholy sound resounded as far as the Dover cliffs, fuelling the rumour that Bonaparte had hired the Devil himself as a look-out.

How did he feel about working for the French?

He preferred it to working for the English.

Without Bonaparte to care for I spent much of my time with Patrick on the pillar. The top of it was about twenty feet by fifteen, so there was room to play cards. Sometimes Domino came up for a boxing match. His unusual height was no disadvantage to him and, although Patrick had fists like cannonballs, he never once landed a blow on Domino, whose tactic was to jump about until his opponent started to tire. Judging his moment, Domino hit once and once only, not with his fists but with both feet, hurling himself sideways or backwards or pushing off from a lightning handstand. These were playful matches, but I've seen him fell an ox simply by leaping at its forehead.

'If you were my size, Henri, you'd learn to look after yourself, you wouldn't rely on the good nature of others.'

Looking out from the pillar I let Patrick describe to me the activity on deck beneath the English sails. He could see the Admirals in their white leggings and the sailors running up and down the rigging, altering the sail to make the most of the wind. There were plenty of floggings. Patrick said he saw a man's back lifted off in one clean piece. They dipped him in the sea to save him from turning septic and left him on deck staring at the sun. Patrick said he could see the weevils in the bread.

Don't believe that one.

July 20th, 1804. Too early for dawn but not night either.

There's a restlessness in the trees, out at sea, in the camp. The birds and we are sleeping fitfully, wanting to be asleep but tense with the idea of awakening. In maybe half an hour, that familiar cold grey light. Then the sun. Then the seagulls crying out over the water. I get up at this time most days. I walk down to the port to watch the ships tethered like dogs.

I wait for the sun to slash the water.

The last nineteen days have been millpond days. We have dried our clothes on the burning stones not pegged them up to the wind, but today my shirt-sleeves are whipping round my arms and the ships are listing badly.

We are on parade today. Bonaparte arrives in a couple of

hours to watch us put out to sea. He wants to launch 25,000 men in fifteen minutes.

He will.

This sudden weather is unexpected. If it worsens it will be impossible to risk the Channel.

Patrick says the Channel is full of mermaids. He says it's the mermaids lonely for a man that pull so many of us down.

Watching the white crests slapping against the sides of the ships, I wonder if this mischief storm is their doing?

Optimistically, it may pass.

Noon. The rain is running off our noses down our jackets into our boots. To talk to the next man I have to cup my hands around my mouth. The wind has already loosened scores of barges, forcing men out chest deep into the impossible waters, making a nonsense of our best knots. The officers say we can't risk a practice today. Bonaparte, with his coat pulled round his head, says we can. We will.

July 20th, 1804. Two thousand men were drowned today.

In gales so strong that Patrick as look-out had to be tied to barrels of apples, we discovered that our barges are children's toys after all. Bonaparte stood on the dockside and told his officers that no storm could defeat us.

'Why, if the heavens fell down we would hold them up on the points of our lances.'

Perhaps. But there's no will and no weapon that can hold back the sea.

I lay next to Patrick, flat and strapped, hardly seeing at all for the spray, but every gap the wind left showed me another gap where a boat had been.

The mermaids won't be lonely any more.

We should have turned on him, should have laughed in his face, should have shook the dead-men-seaweed-hair in his face.

But his face is always pleading with us to prove him right.

At night when the storm had dropped and we were left in sodden tents with steaming bowls of coffee, none of us spoke out.

No one said, Let's leave him, let's hate him. We held our bowls in both hands and drank our coffee with the brandy ration he'd sent specially to every man.

I had to serve him that night and his smile pushed away the madness of arms and legs that pushed in at my ears and mouth.

I was covered in dead men.

In the morning, 2,000 new recruits marched into Boulogne.

Do you ever think of your childhood?

I think of it when I smell porridge. Sometimes after I've been by the docks I walk into town and use my nose tracking fresh bread and bacon. Always, passing a particular house, that sits like the others in a sort of row, and is the same as them, I smell the slow smell of oats. Sweet but with an edge of salt. Thick like a blanket. I don't know who lives in the house, who is responsible, but I imagine the yellow fire and the black pot. At home we used a copper pot that I polished, loving to polish anything that would keep a shine. My mother made porridge, leaving the oats overnight by the old fire. Then in the morning when her bellows work had sent the sparks shooting up the chimney, she burned the oats brown at the sides, so that the sides were like brown paper lining the pot and the inside slopped white over the edge.

We trod on a flag floor but in the winter she put down hay and the hay and the oats made us smell like a manger.

Most of my friends ate hot bread in the mornings.

I was happy but happy is an adult word. You don't have to ask a child about happy, you see it. They are or they are not. Adults talk about being happy because largely they are not. Talking about it is the same as trying to catch the wind. Much easier to let it blow all over you. This is where I disagree with the philosophers. They talk about passionate things but there is no passion in them. Never talk happiness with a philosopher.

But I'm not a child any more and often the Kingdom of Heaven eludes me too. Now, words and ideas will always slip themselves in between me and the feeling. Even our birthright feeling, which is to be happy.

This morning I smell the oats and I see a little boy watching his reflection in a copper pot he's polished. His father comes in and laughs and offers him his shaving mirror instead. But in the shaving mirror the boy can only see one face. In the pot he can see all the distortions of his face. He sees many possible faces and so he sees what he might become.

The recruits have arrived, most without moustaches, all with apples in their cheeks. Fresh country produce like me. Their faces are open and eager. They're being fussed over, given uniforms and duties to replace the yell for the milk pail and the insistent pigs. The officers shake hands with them; a grown-up thing to do.

No one mentions yesterday's parade. We're dry, the tents are drying, the soaked barges are upturned in the dock. The sea is innocent and Patrick on his pillar is shaving quietly. The recruits are being divided into regiments; friends are separated on principle. This is a new start. These boys are men.

What souvenirs they have brought from home will soon be lost or eaten.

Odd, the difference that a few months makes. When I came here I was just like them, still am in many ways, but my companions are no longer the shy boys with cannon-fire in their eyes. They are rougher, tougher. Naturally you say, that's what army life is about.

It's about something else too, something hard to talk about.

When we came here, we came from our mothers and our

sweethearts. We were still used to our mothers with their work-hard arms that could clout the strongest of us and leave our ears ringing. And we courted our sweethearts in the country way. Slow, with the fields that ripen at harvest. Fierce, with the sows that rut the earth. Here, without women, with only our imaginations and a handful of whores, we can't remember what it is about women that can turn a man through passion into something holy. Bible words again, but I am thinking of my father who shaded his eyes on those sunburnt evenings and learned to take his time with my mother. I am thinking of my mother with her noisy heart and of all the women waiting in the fields for the men who drowned yesterday and all the mothers' sons who have taken their place.

We never think of them here. We think of their bodies and now and then we talk about home but we don't think of them as they are; the most solid, the best loved, the well known.

They go on. Whatever we do or undo, they go on.

There was a man in our village who liked to think of himself as an inventor. He spent a lot of time with pulleys and bits of rope and offcuts of wood making devices that could raise a cow or laying pipes to bring the river water right into the house. He was a man with light in his voice and an easy way with his neighbours. Used to disappointment, he could always assuage the disappointment in others. And in a village subject to the rain and sun there are many disappointments.

All the while that he invented and re-invented and cheered us up, his wife, who never spoke except to say, 'Dinner's ready', worked in the fields and kept house and, because the man liked his bed, she was soon bringing up six children too.

Once, he went to town for a few months to try and make his fortune and when he came back with no fortune and without their savings, she was sitting quietly in a clean house mending clean clothes and the fields were planted for another year.

You can tell I liked this man, and I'd be a fool to say he didn't work, that we didn't need him and his optimistic ways. But when she died, suddenly, at noon, the light went out of his voice and his pipes filled with mud and he could hardly harvest his land let alone bring up six children.

She had made him possible. In that sense she was his god. Like God, she was neglected.

New recruits cry when they come here and they think about their mothers and their sweethearts and they think about going home. They remember what it is about home that holds their hearts; not sentiment or show but faces they love. Most of these recruits aren't seventeen and they're asked to do in a few weeks what vexes the best philosophers for a lifetime; that is, to gather up their passion for life and make sense of it in the face of death.

They don't know how but they do know how to forget, and little by little they put aside the burning summer in their bodies and all they have instead is lust and rage.

It was after the disaster at sea that I started to keep a diary. I started so that I wouldn't forget. So that in later life when I was prone to sit by the fire and look back, I'd have something clear and sure to set against my memory tricks. I told Domino; he said, 'The way you see it now is no more real than the way you'll see it then.'

I couldn't agree with him. I knew how old men blurred and lied making the past always the best because it was gone. Hadn't Bonaparte said so himself?

'Look at you,' said Domino, 'a young man brought up by a priest and a pious mother. A young man who can't pick up a musket to shoot a rabbit. What makes you think you can see anything clearly? What gives you the right to make a notebook and shake it at me in thirty years, if we're still alive, and say you've got the truth?'

'I don't care about the facts, Domino, I care about how I feel. How I feel will change, I want to remember that.'

He shrugged and left me. He never talked about the future and only occasionally, when drunk, would he talk about his marvellous past. A past filled with sequined women and double-tailed horses and a father who made his living being fired from a cannon. He came from somewhere in eastern Europe and his skin was the colour of old olives. We only knew he had wandered into France by mistake, years ago, and saved the lady Joséphine from the hooves of a runaway horse. She was plain Madame Beauharnais then, recently out of the slimy prison of Carmes and recently widowed. Her husband had been executed in the Terror; she had only escaped because Robespierre was murdered on the morning she was to follow him. Domino called her a lady of good sense and claimed that in her penniless days she had challenged officers to play her at billiards. If she lost, they could stay to breakfast. If she won, they were to pay one of her more pressing bills.

She never lost.

Years later, she had recommended Domino to her husband eager for a groom he could keep and they had found him eating fire in some sideshow. His loyalties to Bonaparte were mixed, but he loved both Joséphine and the horses.

He told me about the fortune tellers he'd known and how crowds came every week to have their future opened or their past revealed. 'But I tell you, Henri, that every moment you steal from the present is a moment you have lost for ever. There's only now.'

I ignored him and kept working on my little book and in August when the sun turned the grass yellow, Bonaparte announced his Coronation that coming December.

I was given immediate leave. He told me he'd want me with him after that. Told me we were going to do great things. Told me he liked a smiling face with his dinner. It's always been the way with me; either everyone ignores me, or they take me into their confidence. At first I thought it was just priests because priests are more intense than ordinary people. It's not just priests, it must be something about the way I look.

When I started working for Napoleon directly I thought he spoke in aphorisms, he never said a sentence like you or I would, it was put like a great thought. I wrote them all down and only later realised how bizarre most of them were. They were lines from his memorable deliveries and I should admit that I wept when I heard him speak. Even when I hated him, he could still make me cry. And not through fear. He was great. Greatness like his is hard to be sensible about.

It took me a week to get home, riding where I could, walking the rest. News of the Coronation was spreading and I saw in the smiles of the people I travelled with how welcome it was. None of us thought that only fifteen years ago we had fought to do away with Kings for ever. That we had sworn never to fight again except in self-defence. Now we wanted a ruler and we wanted him to rule the world. We are not an unusual people.

In my soldier's uniform I was treated with kindness, fed and cared for, given the pick of the harvest. In return I told stories about the camp at Boulogne and how we could see the English quaking in their boots on the opposite shore. I embroidered and invented and even lied. Why not? It made them happy. I didn't talk about the men who have married mermaids. All the farm lads wanted to join up straight away, but I advised them to wait until after the Coronation.

'When your Emperor needs you, he'll call. Until then, work for France at home.'

Naturally, this pleased the women.

I had been away six months. When the cart I was riding in dropped me a mile or so from home I felt like turning back. I was afraid. Afraid that things would be different, that I wouldn't be welcome. The traveller always wants home to be just as it was. The traveller expects to change, to return with a bushy beard or a new baby or tales of a miraculous life where the streams are full of gold and the weather is gentle. I was full of such stories, but I wanted to know in advance that my audience was seated. Skirting the obvious track, I crept up on my village like a bandit. I had already decided what they should be doing. That my mother would be just visible in the potato field, that my father would be in the cowshed. I was going to run down the hill and then we'd have a party. They didn't know to expect me. No message could have reached them in a week.

I looked. They were both in the fields. My mother with her hands on her hips, head pushed back, watching the clouds gather. She was expecting rain. She was making her plans in accordance with the rain. Beside her, my father stood still, holding a sack in each hand. When I was small, I'd seen my father with two sacks like that, but they had been full of blind moles, their whiskers still rough with dirt. They were dead. We trapped them because they ruined the fields but I didn't know that then, I only knew that my father had killed them. It was my mother who pulled me away rigid with cold from my night vigil. In the morning the sacks were gone. I've killed them myself since, but only by looking the other way.

Mother. Father. I love you.

We stayed up late so many nights drinking Claude's rough cognac and sitting till the fire was the colour of fading roses. My mother talked about her past with gaiety, she seemed to believe that with a ruler on the throne much would be restored. She even talked about writing to her parents. She knew they'd be celebrating the return of a monarch. I was surprised, I thought she'd always supported the Bourbons. Becoming an Emperor didn't make this man she'd hated into a man she could love surely?

'He's doing right, Henri. A country needs a King and a Queen, otherwise who are we to look up to?'

'You can look up to Bonaparte. King or not.'

But she couldn't. He knew she couldn't. It was not simple vanity that was putting this man on the throne.

When my mother talked about her parents, she harboured the same hopes as the traveller who returns home. She thought of them unchanged, described the furniture as though nothing would have been moved or broken in more than twenty years. Her father's beard was still the same colour. I understood her hopes. We all had something to pin on Bonaparte.

Time is a great deadener. People forget, grow old, get bored. The mother and father she'd risked her life to escape from she now spoke of with affection. Had she forgotten? Had time worn away her anger?

She looked at me. 'I'm not so greedy as I get older, Henri. I take what there is and I've stopped asking questions about where it comes from. It gives me pleasure to think of them. It gives me pleasure to love them. That's all.'

My face burned. What right had I to challenge her? To take the light out of her eyes and make her think of herself as foolish and sentimental? I knelt in front of her, my back to the fire, my chest resting against her knees. She kept hold of her darning. 'You're like I was,' she said. 'No patience with a weak heart.'

It rained for days. Thin rain that soaked you in half an hour without the thrill of a real torrent. I went from home to home gossiping and seeing friends, helping with whatever had to be mended or gathered. My friend the priest was on a pilgrimage, so I left him long letters of the kind I would most like to receive.

I like the early dark. It's not night. It's still companionable. No one feels afraid to walk by themselves without a lantern. The girls sing on their way back from the last milking and if I jump out on them they'll shout and chase me but there'll be no pounding hearts. I don't know why it is that one kind of dark can be so different from another. Real dark is thicker and quieter, it fills up the space between your jacket and your heart. It gets in your eyes. When I have to be out late at night, it's not knives and kicks I'm afraid of, though there are plenty of those behind walls and hedges. I'm afraid of the Dark. You, who walk  so cheerfully, whistling your way, stand still for five minutes. Stand still in the Dark in a field or down a track. It's then you know you're there on sufferance. The Dark only lets you take one step at a time. Step and the Dark closes round your back. In front, there is no space for you until you take it. Darkness is absolute. Walking in the Dark is like swimming underwater except you can't come up for air.

Lie still at night and Dark is soft to the touch, it's made of moleskin and is such a sweet smotherer. In the country we rely on the moon, and when the moon is out no light can penetrate the window. The window is walled over and cast in a perfect black surface. Does it feel the same to be blind? I used to think so, but I've been told not. A blind pedlar who visited us regularly laughed at my stories of the Dark and said the Dark was his wife. We bought our pails from him and fed him in the kitchen. He never spilt his stew or missed his mouth the way I did. 'I can see,' he said, 'but I don't use my eyes.'

He died last winter, my mother said.

It's early dark now and this is the last night of my leave. We won't do anything unusual. We don't want to think that I'm going again.

I have promised my mother that she will come to Paris soon after the Coronation. I've never been myself and it's the thought of that that makes it easier for me to say goodbye. Domino will be there grooming his preposterous horse, teaching the mad beast to walk in a quiet line with Court animals. Why Bonaparte has insisted on having that horse present at such an important time is not clear. It's a soldier's mount, not a creature for parades. But he's always reminding us that he's a soldier too.

When Claude had finally gone to bed and we were alone, we didn't talk. We held hands until the wick burnt out and then we were in the dark.

Paris had never seen so much money.

The Bonapartes were ordering everything from cream to David. David, who had flattered Napoleon by calling his head perfectly Roman, was given the commission to paint the Coronation, and he was to be found each day at Notre-Dame making cartoons and arguing with the workmen who were trying to do away with the ravages of revolution and bankruptcy. Joséphine, given charge of the flowers, had not contented herself with vases and arrangements. She had drawn up a plan of the route to the cathedral from the palace and was engaged as intently as David on her own ephemeral masterpiece. I first encountered her over the billiard table, where she was playing Monsieur Talleyrand, a gentleman not gifted with balls. In spite of her dress, which spread out would easily have made a carpet all the way to the cathedral, she bent and moved as though she wore nothing at all, making beautiful parallel lines with her cue. Bonaparte had dressed me up as a footman and ordered me to take her Highness an afternoon snack. She was fond of melon at four o'clock. Monsieur Talleyrand was to have port.

This holiday mood of Napoleon's was almost a madness. He had appeared at dinner two nights ago dressed as the Pontiff and lewdly asked Joséphine how intimate she would like to be with God. I stared into the chicken.

Now, he had me out of my soldier's uniform and in Court dress. Impossibly tight. It made him laugh. He liked to laugh. It was his only relaxation apart from those hotter and hotter baths he took at any time of the day or night. In the palace the bathroom staff lived in the same state of unrest as the kitchen staff. He might cry out for hot water at any moment, and woe betide the man on duty if the tub were not just full, just so. I'd only seen the bathroom once. A great big room with a tub the size of a line-ship and a huge furnace in one corner, where the water was heated and drawn and poured back and reheated over and over again until the moment came and he wanted it. The attendants were specially chosen from amongst the best ox-wrestlers in France. Fellows who could handle the copper kettles like tea-cups worked alone, stripped to the waist, wearing only sailor's breeches that caught the sweat and held it in dark stripes down each leg. Like sailors they had their liquor ration, but I don't know what it was made of. The biggest, André, offered me a swig from his flask the time I poked my head round the door, gasping at the steam and this huge man who looked like a genie. I accepted out of politeness, but spat the brown stuff over the tiles, frantic at the heat. He pinched my arm the way the cook pinched spaghetti strings and told me that the hotter it is the hotter the liquid you drink.

'Why do you think they drink all that rum in Martinique?' and he winked broadly, imitating her Highness's walk. Now, here she was before me and I was too shy to announce the melon.

Talleyrand coughed.

'I won't miss because you grunt,' she said.

He coughed again and she looked up, and seeing me standing there put down her cue and moved to take away my tray.

'I know all the servants, but I don't know you.'

'I'm from Boulogne, Majesty. I've come to serve the chicken.'

She laughed and her eyes travelled up and down my person.

'You don't dress like a soldier.'

'No, Majesty. My orders were to dress as Court now that I'm at Court.'

She nodded. 'I think you might dress any way you like. I'll ask him for you. Wouldn't you prefer to wait on me? Melon is so much sweeter than chicken.'

I was horrified. Had I come all this way just to lose him?

'No, Majesty. I couldn't do melon. I can only do chicken. I've been trained.'

(I sound like a street urchin.)

Her hand rested on my arm for a second, and her eyes were keen.

'I can see how zealous you are. Go now.'

Thankfully I bowed out backwards and ran down to the servants' hall, where I had a little room of my own; the privilege of being a special attendant. I kept my few books there, a flute I was hoping to learn and my journal. I wrote about her or tried to. She eluded me the way the tarts in Boulogne had eluded me. I decided to write about Napoleon instead.

After that, I was kept busy with banquet after banquet as all our conquered territories came to congratulate the Emperor to be. While the guests filled themselves on rare fish and veal in newly invented sauces, he kept to his chicken, eating a whole one every night, usually forgetting about the vegetables. No one ever mentioned it. He only needed to cough and the table fell silent. Now and again I caught her Majesty watching me, but if our eyes met, she smiled in that half way of hers and I dropped my eyes. Even to look at her was to wrong him. She belonged to him. I envied her that.

In the weeks that followed he grew morbidly afraid of being poisoned or assassinated, not for himself, but because the future of France was at stake. He had me taste all his food before he would touch it and he doubled his guard. Rumour had it that he even checked his bed before he slept. Not that he slept much. He was like a dog, he could close his eyes and snore in a moment, but when his mind was full he was able to stay awake for days while his Generals and friends dropped around him.

Abruptly, at the end of November and only two weeks from

his Coronation, he ordered me back to Boulogne. He said I lacked a real soldier's training, that I would serve him better when I could handle a musket as well as a carving knife. Perhaps he saw how I blushed, perhaps he knew my feelings, he knew those of most people. He tweaked my ear in his maddening way and promised there was a special job for me in the New Year.

So I left the city of dreams just as it was about to flower and heard second-hand reports of that gaudy morning when Napoleon had taken the crown from the Pope and placed it on his own head before crowning Joséphine. They say that he bought Madame Clicquot's entire stock for the whole year. With her husband lately dead and the whole weight of the business on her shoulders, she can only have blessed the return of a King. She was not alone. Paris threw open every door and lit every chandelier for three days. Only the old and ill bothered to go to bed, for the rest it was drunkenness and madness and joy. (I exclude the aristocrats, but they are not relevant.)

In Boulogne, in the terrible weather, I trained for ten hours a day and collapsed at night in a damp bivouac with a couple of inadequate blankets. Our supplies and conditions had always been good, but in my absence thousands more men had joined up, believing through the offices of Napoleon's fervent clergy that the road to Heaven was first the road to Boulogne. No one was exempt from conscription. It was up to the recruiting officers to decide who should stay and who must go. By Christmas, the camp had swelled to over 100,000 men and more were expected. We ran with packs that weighed around 40 lbs, waded in and out of the sea, fought one another hand to hand and used all the available farming land to feed ourselves. Even so, it was not enough and, in spite of Napoleon's dislike of supply contractors, we got most of our meat from nameless regions and I suspect from animals that Adam would not recognise. Two pounds of bread, 4 oz of meat and 4 oz of vegetables were rationed to us daily. We stole what we could, spent our wages, when we had them, on tavern food and wreaked havoc on the communities who lived quietly round about. Napoleon himself ordered *vivandières* to be sent to special camps. *Vivandière* is an optimistic army word. He sent tarts who had no reason to be *vivant* about anything. Their food was often worse than ours, they had us as many hours of the day as we could stand and the pay was poor. The well-padded town tarts took pity on them and were often to be seen visiting the camps with blankets and loaves of bread. The *vivandières* were runaways, strays, younger daughters of too-large families, servant girls who'd got tired of giving it away to drunken masters, and fat old dames who couldn't ply their trade anywhere else. On arrival they were each given a set of underclothes and a dress that chilled their bosoms in the icy sea-salt days. Shawls were distributed too, but any woman found covering herself on duty could be reported and fined. Fined meant no money that week instead of hardly any money. Unlike the town tarts, who protected themselves and charged what they liked and certainly charged individually, the *vivants* were expected to service as many men as asked them day or night. One woman I met crawling home after an officer's party said she'd lost count at thirty-nine.

Christ lost consciousness at thirty-nine.

Most of us that winter got great sores where the salt and wind had rubbed down our skin. Sores between our toes and on our top lips were the most common. A moustache didn't help, the hairs aggravated the rawness.

At Christmas, though the *vivandières* had no time off, we did, and we sat around our fires with extra logs toasting the Emperor with our extra brandy. Patrick and I feasted on a goose I stole, cooking and eating it in guilty joy on top of his pillar. We should have shared it, but as it was we were still hungry. He told me stories about Ireland, about the peat fires and the goblins that live under every hill.

'Sure and I've had my own boots made the size of a thumbnail by the little people.'

He said he'd been out poaching, that it was a fine night in July, just dark, with the moon up and a great stretch of stars. As he came through the wood he saw a ring of green fire burning as tall as a man. In the middle of the ring were three goblins. He knew they were goblins and not elves by their shovels and beards. 'So I kept as quiet as the church bell on a Saturday night and crept up to them as you would a pheasant.'

He had heard them discussing their treasure, stolen from the fairies and buried under the ground within the ring of fire. Suddenly one of the goblins had put his nose to the air and sniffed suspiciously.

'I smell a man,' he said. 'A dirty man with mud on his boots.' Another laughed. 'What does it matter? No one with mud on his boots can enter our secret chamber.'

'Take no chances, let's be off,' said the first and in a wink they were gone, ring of fire with them. For a few moments Patrick lay still among the leaves turning over what he had heard. Then, checking he was alone, he took off his boots and crept to where the ring of fire had been. On the ground there was no sign of burning but the soles of his feet tingled.

'So I knew I was in a magic place.'

He had dug all night and in the morning found nothing but a couple of moles and a pile of worms. Exhausted, he had gone back for his boots and there they were.

'No bigger than a thumbnail.'

He searched his pockets and handed me a tiny pair of boots, perfectly made, the heels worn down and the laces frayed.

'An' I swear they fitted me once.'

I didn't know whether to believe him or not and he saw my eyebrows working up and down. He held out his hand for the boots. 'I walked all the way home in my bare feet and when I came to take Mass that morning I could hardly hobble up to the altar. I was so tired that I gave the congregation the day off.' He smiled his crooked smile and hit me on the shoulder.

'Trust me, I'm telling you stories.'

He told me other stories too. Stories about the Blessed Virgin and how she couldn't be relied upon.

'The women, they're always the clever ones,' he said.

'They always sense our lying ways. The Blessed Virgin's a woman too, for all that she's Holy, and there's no man I know can get his own way with her. You can pray all day and all night and she won't hear you. If you're a man, you'd much better stick with Jesus himself.'

I said something about how the Blessed Virgin was our mediator.

'Sure she is, but she mediates for the women. Why, we've a statue at home, so lifelike you'd think it was the Holy Mother herself. Now the women come in with their tears and flowers and I've hidden behind a pillar and I'll swear on all the saints that the statue moves. Now when the men come in, cap in hand, asking for this and that and saying their prayers, that statue's like the rock it's made of. I've given them the truth over and over again. Go straight to Jesus, I say (he's got a statue near by), but they don't heed because every man likes to think he's got a woman listening to him.'

'Don't you pray to her?'

'Sure an' I do not. We have an arrangement you might say. I see to her, give her proper respect and we leave each other alone. She'd be different if God hadn't violated her.'

What was he talking about?

'See, women like you to treat them with respect. To ask before you touch. Now I've never thought it was right and proper of God to send his angel with no by your leave and then have his way before she'd even had time to comb her hair. I don't think she ever forgave him for that. He was too hasty. So I don't blame her that she's so haughty now.'

I had never thought of the Queen of Heaven in this way.

Patrick liked the girls and was not above sneaking a look uninvited.

'But when it comes to it, I'd never take a woman without giving her time to comb her hair.'

We spent the rest of our Christmas leave on top of the pillar sheltering behind the apple barrels and playing cards. But on New Year's Eve Patrick swung out his ladder and said we were to go to Communion.

'I'm not a believer.'

'Then you'll come as my friend.'

He cajoled me with a bottle of brandy for afterwards and so we set off through the frozen streets to the seaman's church that Patrick preferred to army prayers.

It was filling slowly with men and women from the town, muffled against the cold but in the best clothes they could find. We were the only ones from the camp. Probably the only ones still sober in this desperate weather. The church was plain except for the coloured windows and the statue of the Queen of Heaven decked in red robes. Despite myself I made her a little bow and Patrick, catching me, smiled his crooked smile.

We sang with our strongest voices and the warmth and nearness of other people thawed my unbeliever's heart and I too saw God through the frost. The plain windows were trellised with frost and the stone floor that received our knees had the coldness of the grave. The oldest were dignified with smiling faces and the children, some of whom were so poor that they kept their hands warm in bandages, grew angel hair.

The Queen of Heaven looked down.

When we had put aside our stained prayer books that only some of us could read we took communion with clean hearts, and Patrick, who had clipped his moustache, whipped to the end of the queue and managed to receive the host twice.

'Double the blessing,' he whispered to me.

I had not intended to take communion at all, but my longing for strong arms and certainty and the quiet holiness around me forced me to my feet and down the aisle where strangers met my eyes as though I had been their son. Kneeling, with the incense making me light-headed and the slow repetition of the priest calming my banging heart, I thought again about a life with God, thought of my mother, who would now be kneeling too, far away and cupping her hands for her portion of the Kingdom. In my village, each house would be empty and silent but the barn would be full. Full of honest people who had no church making a church out of themselves. Their flesh and blood.

The patient cattle sleep.

I took the wafer on my tongue and it burned my tongue. The wine tasted of dead men, 2,000 dead men. In the face of the priest I saw dead men accusing me. I saw tents sodden at dawn. I saw women with blue breasts. I gripped the chalice, though I could feel the priest try and take it from me.

I gripped the chalice.

When the priest gently curled away my fingers I saw the imprint of the silver on each palm. Were these my stigmata then? Would I bleed for every death and living death? If a soldier did, there would be no soldiers left. We would go under the hill with the goblins. We would marry the mermaids. We would never leave our homes.

I left Patrick at his second communion and went out into the freezing night. It was not yet twelve. No bells were ringing, no flares were lit, heralding a new year and praising God and the Emperor.

This year is gone, I told myself. This year is slipping away and it will never return. Domino's right, there's only now. Forget it. Forget it. You can't bring it back. You can't bring them back.

They say that every snowflake is different. If that were true, how could the world go on? How could we ever get up off our knees? How could we ever recover from the wonder of it?

By forgetting. We cannot keep in mind too many things.
There is only the present and nothing to remember.

On the flagstones, still visible under a coating of ice, some child had scrawled a game of noughts and crosses in red tailor's chalk. You play, you win, you play, you lose. You play. It's the playing that's irresistible. Dicing from one year to the next with the things you love, what you risk reveals what you value. I sat down and scratching in the ice drew my own square of innocent noughts and angry crosses. Perhaps the Devil would partner me. Perhaps the Queen of Heaven. Napoleon, Joséphine. Does it matter whom you lose to, if you lose?

From the church came the roar of the last hymn.

Not heard as half-hearted hymns are heard on monotonous Sundays when the congregation would rather be in bed or with their sweethearts. This was no lukewarm appeal to an exacting God but love and confidence that hung in the rafters, pushed open the church door, forced the cold from the stone, forced the stones to cry out. The church vibrated.

My soul doth magnify the Lord.

What gave them this joy?

What made cold and hungry people so sure that another year could only be better? Was it Him, Him on the throne? Their little Lord in his simple uniform?

What does it matter? Why do I question what I see to be real?

Down the street towards me comes a woman with wild hair, her boots making sparks orange against the ice. She's laughing. She's holding a baby very close. She comes straight to me.

'Happy New Year, soldier.'

Her baby is wide awake with clear blue eyes and curious fingers that move from buttons to nose to stretch at me. I wrap my arms around them both and we make a strange shape swaying slightly near the wall. The hymn is over and the moment of silence takes me by surprise.

The baby burps.

Then the flares go out across the Channel and a great cheer from our camp two miles away comes clearly to where we stand. The woman pulls away, kisses me and disappears with her sparking heels. Queen of Heaven, go with her.

Here they come, with the Lord sewn in their hearts for another year. Arm in arm, huddled together, some running, some walking with long strides like wedding guests. The priest is at the door of the church, standing in a pool of light and beside him, the altar boys in their scarlet, shelter the holy candles from the wind. From across the street where I am standing I can see through the door, down the aisle and up to the altar. The church is empty now, except for Patrick, who is standing with his back to me right up against the altar rail. By the time he comes out, the bells are ringing crazily and at least a dozen women whom I've never met have thrown their arms around my neck and blessed me. Most of the men are in groups of five or six, still by the church, but the women are joining hands and making a great circle that blocks the road and fills the space from one side of the street to the other. They start to dance, going round and round faster and faster until my eyes are dizzy with keeping up with them. I don't recognise their song but their voices are full.

Sequester my heart.

Wherever love is, I want to be, I will follow it as surely as the land-locked salmon finds the sea.

'Drink this,' said Patrick, pushing a bottle towards me. 'You won't taste the like again.'

'Where did you get it?' I smelled the cork, it was round and ripe and sensual.

'From behind the altar. They always keep a good drop for themselves.'

We walked the miles back to the camp, meeting a band of soldiers carrying one who'd thrown himself into the sea as a New Year gesture. He wasn't dead, but he was too cold to speak. They were taking him to a brothel to get warm. Soldiers and women. That's how the world is. Any other role is temporary. Any other role is a gesture.

We slept in the kitchen tent that night as a concession to the unimaginable zero temperature. Unfeelable too. The body shuts down when it has too much to bear; goes its own way quietly inside, waiting for a better time, leaving you numb and half alive. With frosty bodies all about us, drunken men sleeping off another year, we finished the wine and the brandy and shoved our feet under the potato sacks, boots off, but nothing else. I listened to Patrick's regular breathing choke into a snore. He was lost in his world of goblins and treasure, always sure that he would find treasure, even if it was only a bottle of claret from behind the altar. Perhaps the Queen of Heaven did care for him.

I lay awake till the seagulls began to cry. It was New Year's Day, 1805, and I was twenty.

· 2 ·

the Queen of Spades

There is a city surrounded by water with watery alleys that do for streets and roads and silted up back ways that only the rats can cross. Miss your way, which is easy to do, and you may find yourself staring at a hundred eyes guarding a filthy palace of sacks and bones. Find your way, which is easy to do, and you may meet an old woman in a doorway. She will tell your fortune, depending on your face.

This is the city of mazes. You may set off from the same place to the same place every day and never go by the same route. If you do so, it will be by mistake. Your bloodhound nose will not serve you here. Your course in compass reading will fail you. Your confident instructions to passers-by will send them to squares they have never heard of, over canals not listed in the notes.

Although wherever you are going is always in front of you, there is no such thing as straight ahead. No as the crow flies short cut will help you to reach the café just over the water. The short cuts are where the cats go, through the impossible gaps, round corners that seem to take you the opposite way. But here, in this mercurial city, it is required you do awake your faith. With faith, all things are possible.

Rumour has it that the inhabitants of this city walk on water. That, more bizarre still, their feet are webbed. Not all feet, but the feet of the boatmen whose trade is hereditary.

This is the legend.

When a boatman's wife finds herself pregnant she waits until the moon is full and the night empty of idlers. Then she takes her husband's boat and rows to a terrible island where the dead are buried. She leaves her boat with rosemary in the bows so that the limbless ones cannot return with her and hurries to the grave of the most recently dead in her family. She has brought her offerings: a flask of wine, a lock of hair from her husband and a silver coin. She must leave the offerings on the grave and beg for a clean heart if her child be a girl and boatman's feet if her child be a boy. There is no time to lose. She must be home before dawn and the boat must be left for a day and a night covered in salt. In this way, the boatmen keep their secrets and their trade. No newcomer can compete. And no boatman will take off his boots, no matter how you bribe him. I have seen tourists throw diamonds to the fish, but I have never seen a boatman take off his boots.

There was once a weak and foolish man whose wife cleaned the boat and sold the fish and brought up their children and went to the terrible island as she should when her yearly time was due. Their house was hot in summer and cold in winter and there was too little food and too many mouths. This boatman, ferrying a tourist from one church to another, happened to fall into conversation with the man and the man brought up the question of the webbed feet. At the same time he drew a purse of gold from his pocket and let it lie quietly in the bottom of the boat. Winter was approaching, the boatman was thin and he thought what harm could it do to unlace just one boot and let this visitor see what there was. The next morning, the boat was picked up by a couple of priests on their way to Mass. The tourist was babbling incoherently and pulling at his toes with his fingers. There was no boatman. They took the tourist to the madhouse, San Servelo, a quiet place that caters for the well-off and defective. For all I know, he's still there.

And the boatman?

He was my father.

I never knew him because I wasn't born when he disappeared.

A few weeks after my mother had been left with an empty boat she discovered she was pregnant. Although her future was uncertain and she wasn't strictly speaking married to a boatman any more, she decided to go ahead with the gloomy ritual, and on the appropriate night she rowed her way silently across the lagoon. As she fastened the boat, an owl flew very low and caught her on the shoulder with its wing. She was not hurt but she cried out and stepped back and, as she did so, dropped the sprig of rosemary into the sea. For a moment she thought of returning straight away but, crossing herself, she hurried to her father's grave and placed her offerings. She knew her husband should have been the one, but he had no grave. How like him, she thought, to be as absent in death as he was in life. Her deed done, she pushed off from the shore that even the crabs avoided and later covered the boat in so much salt that it sank.

The Blessed Virgin must have protected her. Even before I was born she had married again. This time, a prosperous baker who could afford to take Sundays off.

The hour of my birth coincided with an eclipse of the sun and my mother did her best to slow down her labour until it had passed. But I was as impatient then as I am now and I forced my head out while the midwife was downstairs heating some milk. A fine head with a crop of red hair and a pair of eyes that made up for the sun's eclipse.

A girl.

It was an easy birth and the midwife held me upside down by the ankles until I bawled. But it was when they spread me out to dry that my mother fainted and the midwife felt forced to open another bottle of wine.

My feet were webbed.

There never was a girl whose feet were webbed in the entire history of the boatmen. My mother in her swoon had visions of rosemary and blamed herself for her carelessness. Or perhaps it was her carefree pleasure with the baker she should blame herself for? She hadn't thought of my father since his boat had sunk. She hadn't thought of him much while it was afloat. The midwife took out her knife with the thick blade and proposed to cut off the offending parts straight away. My mother weakly nodded, imagining I would feel no pain or that pain for a moment would be better than embarrassment for a lifetime. The midwife tried to make an incision in the translucent triangle between my first two toes but her knife sprang from the skin leaving no mark. She tried again and again in between all the toes on each foot. She bent the point of the knife, but that was all.

'It's the Virgin's will,' she said at last, finishing the bottle. 'There's no knife can get through that.'

My mother started to weep and wail and continued in this way until my stepfather came home. He was a man of the world and not easily put off by a pair of webbed feet.

'No one will see so long as she wears shoes and when it comes to a husband, why it won't be the feet ne'll be interested in.'

This comforted my mother somewhat and we passed the next eighteen years in a normal family way.

Since Bonaparte captured our city of mazes in 1797, we've more or less abandoned ourselves to pleasure. What else is there to do when you've lived a proud and free life and suddenly you're not proud and free any more? We became an enchanted island for the mad, the rich, the bored, the perverted. Our glory days were behind us but our excess was just beginning. That man demolished our churches on a whim and looted our treasures. That woman of his has jewels in her crown that come out of St Mark's. But of all sorrows, he has our living horses cast by men who stretched their arms between the Devil and God and imprisoned life in a brazen form. He took them from the Basilica and has thrown them up in some readymade square in that tart of towns, Paris.

There were four churches that I loved, which stood looking out across the lagoon to the quiet islands that lie about us. He tore them down to make a public garden. Why did we want a public garden? And if we had and if we had chosen it ourselves we would never have filled it with hundreds of pines laid out in regimental rows. They say Joséphine's a botanist. Couldn't she have found us something a little more exotic? I don't hate the French. My father likes them. They've made his business thrive with their craving for foolish cakes.

He gave me a French name too.

Villanelle. It's pretty enough.

I don't hate the French. I ignore them.

When I was eighteen I started to work the Casino. There aren't many jobs for a girl. I didn't want to go into the bakery and grow old with red hands and forearms like thighs. I couldn't be a dancer, for obvious reasons, and what I would have most liked to have done, worked the boats, was closed to me on account of my sex.

I did take a boat out sometimes, rowing alone for hours up and down the canals and out into the lagoon. I learned the secret ways of boatmen, by watching and by instinct.

If ever I saw a stern disappearing down a black, inhospitable-looking waterway, I followed it and discovered the city within the city that is the knowledge of a few. In this inner city are thieves and Jews and children with slant eyes who come from the eastern wastelands without father or mother. They roam in packs like the cats and the rats and they go after the same food. No one knows why they are here or on what sinister vessel they arrived. They seem to die at twelve or thirteen and yet they are always replaced. I've watched them take a knife to each other for a filthy pile of chicken.

There are exiles too. Men and women driven out of their gleaming palaces that open so elegantly on to shining canals. Men and women who are officially dead according to the registers of Paris. They're here, with the odd bit of gold plate stuffed in a bag as they fled. So long as the Jews will buy the plate and the plate holds out, they survive. When you see the floating corpses belly upwards, you know the gold is ended.

One woman who kept a fleet of boats and a string of cats and dealt in spices lives here now, in the silent city. I cannot tell how old she may be, her hair is green with slime from the walls of the nook she lives in. She feeds on vegetable matter that snags against the stones when the tide is sluggish. She has no teeth. She has no need of teeth. She still wears the curtains that she dragged from her drawing-room window as she left. One curtain she wraps round herself and the other she drapes over her shoulders like a cloak. She sleeps like this.

I've spoken to her. When she hears a boat go by her head pokes out of her nook and she asks you what time of day it might be. Never what time it is; she's too much of a philosopher for that. I saw her once, at evening, her ghoulish hair lit by a lamp she has. She was spreading pieces of rancid meat on a cloth. There were wine goblets beside her.

'I'm having guests to dinner,' she shouted, as I glided past on the other side. 'I would have invited you, but I don't know your name.'

'Villanelle,' I shouted back.

'You're a Venetian, but you wear your name as a disguise. Beware the dice and games of chance.'

She turned back to her cloth and, although we met again, she never used my name, nor gave any sign that she recognised me.

I went to work in the Casino, raking dice and spreading cards and lifting wallets where I could. There was a cellarful of champagne drunk every night and a cruel dog kept hungry to deal with anyone who couldn't pay. I dressed as a boy because that's what the visitors liked to see. It was part of the game, trying to decide which sex was hidden behind tight breeches and extravagant face-paste . . .

It was August. Bonaparte's birthday and a hot night. We were due for a celebration ball in the Piazza San Marco, though what we Venetians had to celebrate was not clear. In keeping with our customs, the ball was to be fancy dress and the Casino was arranging outdoor gaming tables and booths of chance. Our city swarmed with French and Austrian pleasure-seekers, the usual bewildered stream of English and even a party of Russians intent on finding satisfaction. Satisfying our guests is what we do best. The price is high but the pleasure is exact.

I made up my lips with vermilion and overlaid my face with white powder. I had no need to add a beauty spot, having one of my own in just the right place. I wore my yellow Casino breeches with the stripe down each side of the leg and a pirate's shirt that concealed my breasts. This was required, but the moustache I added was for my own amusement. And perhaps for my own protection. There are too many dark alleys and too many drunken hands on festival nights.

Across our matchless square that Bonaparte had contemptuously called the finest drawing-room in Europe, our engineers had rigged a wooden frame alive with gunpowder. This was to be triggered at midnight and I was optimistic that, with so many heads looking up, so many pockets would be vulnerable.

The ball began at eight o'clock and I began my night drawing cards in the booth of chance.

Queen of spades you win, Ace of clubs you lose. Play again. What will you risk? Your watch? Your house? Your mistress? I like to smell the urgency on them. Even the calmest, the richest, have that smell. It's somewhere between fear and sex. Passion I suppose.

There's a man who comes to play Chance with me most nights at the Casino. A large man with pads of flesh on his palms like baker's dough. When he squeezes my neck from behind, the sweat on his palms makes them squeak. I always carry a handkerchief. He wears a green waistcoat and I've seen him stripped to that waistcoat because he can't let the dice roll without following it. He has funds. He must have. He spends in a moment what I earn in a month. He's cunning though, for all his madness at the table. Most men wear their pockets or their purses on their sleeves when they're drunk. They want everyone to know how rich they are, how fat with gold. Not him. He has a bag down his trousers and he dips into it with his back turned. I'll never pick that one.

I don't know what else might be down there.

He wonders the same thing about me. I catch him staring at my crotch and now and again I wear a codpiece to taunt him. My breasts are small, so there's no cleavage to give me away, and I'm tall for a girl, especially a Venetian.

I wonder what he'd say to my feet.

Tonight, he's wearing his best suit and his moustache gleams. I fan the cards before him; close them, shuffle them, fan them again. He chooses. Too low to win. Choose again. Too high. Forfeit. He laughs and tosses a coin across the counter.

'You've grown a moustache since two days ago.'

'I come from a hairy family.'

'It suits you.' His eyes stray as usual, but I am firmly behind the booth. He takes out another coin. I spread. The Jack of hearts. An ill-omened card but he doesn't think so, he promises to return and taking the Jack with him for luck moves over to the gaming table. His bottom strains his jacket. They're always taking the cards. I wonder whether to get out another pack or just cheat the next customer. I think that will depend on who the next customer might be.

I love the night. In Venice, a long time ago, when we had our own calendar and stayed aloof from the world, we began the days at night. What use was the sun to us when our trade and our secrets and our diplomacy depended on darkness? In the dark you are in disguise and this is the city of disguises. In those days (I cannot place them in time because time is to do with daylight), in those days when the sun went down we opened our doors and slid along the eely waters with a hooded light in our prow. All our boats were black then and left no mark on the water where they sat. We were dealing in perfume and silk. Emeralds and diamonds. Affairs of State. We didn't build our bridges simply to avoid walking on water. Nothing so obvious. A bridge is a meeting place. A neutral place. A casual place. Enemies will choose to meet on a bridge and end their quarrel in that void. One will cross to the other side. The other will not return. For lovers, a bridge is a possibility, a metaphor of their chances. And for the traffic in whispered goods, where else but a bridge in the night?

We are a philosophical people, conversant with the nature of greed and desire, holding hands with the Devil and God. We would not wish to let go of either. This living bridge is tempting to all and you may lose your soul or find it here.

And our own souls?

They are Siamese.

Nowadays, the dark has more light than in the old days. There are flares everywhere and soldiers like to see the streets lit up, like to see some reflection on the canals. They don't trust our soft feet and thin knives. None the less, darkness can be found; in the under-used waterways or out on the lagoon. There's no dark like it. It's soft to the touch and heavy in the hands. You can open your mouth and let it sink into you till it makes a close ball in your belly. You can juggle with it, dodge it, swim in it. You can open it like a door.

The old Venetians had eyes like cats that cut the densest night and took them through impenetrable ways without stumbling. Even now, if you look at us closely you will find that some of us have slit eyes in the daylight.

I used to think that darkness and death were probably the same. That death was the absence of light. That death was nothing more than the shadow-lands where people bought and sold and loved as usual but with less conviction. The night seems more temporary than the day, especially to lovers, and it also seems more uncertain. In this way it sums up our lives, which are uncertain and temporary. We forget about that in the day.

In the day we go on for ever. This is the city of uncertainty, where routes and faces look alike and are not. Death will be like that. We will be forever recognising people we have never met.

But darkness and death are not the same.

The one is temporary, the other is not.

Our funerals are fabulous affairs. We hold them at night, returning to our dark roots. The black boats skim the water and the coffin is crossed with jet. From my upper window that overlooks two intersecting canals, I once saw a rich man's cortège of fifteen boats (the number must be odd) glide out to the lagoon. At the same moment, a pauper's boat, carrying a coffin not varnished but covered in pitch, floated out too, rowed by an old woman with scarcely enough strength to drag the oars. I thought they would collide, but the rich man's boatmen pulled away. Then his widow motioned with her hand and the cortège opened the line at the eleventh boat and made room for the pauper, tossing a rope round the prow so that the old woman had only to guide her craft. They continued thus towards the terrible island of San Michele and I lost sight of them.

For myself, if I am to die, I would like to do it alone, far from the world. I would like to lie on the warm stone in May until my strength is gone, then drop gently into the canal. Such things are still possible in Venice.

Nowadays, the night is designed for the pleasure-seekers and tonight, by their reckoning, is a *tour de force*. There are fire-eaters frothing at the mouth with yellow tongues. There is a dancing bear. There is a troupe of little girls, their sweet bodies hairless and pink, carrying sugared almonds in copper dishes. There are women of every kind and not all of them are women. In the centre of the square, the workers on Murano have fashioned a huge glass slipper that is constantly filled and re-filled with champagne. To drink from it you must lap like a dog and how these visitors love it. One has already drowned, but what is one death in the midst of so much life?

From the wooden frame above where the gunpowder waits there are also suspended a number of nets and trapezes. From here acrobats swing over the square, casting grotesque shadows on the dancers below. Now and again, one will dangle by the knees and snatch a kiss from whoever is standing below. I like such kisses. They fill the mouth and leave the body free. To kiss well one must kiss solely. No groping hands or stammering hearts. The lips and the lips alone are the pleasure. Passion is sweeter split strand by strand. Divided and re-divided like mercury then gathered up only at the last moment.

You see, I am no stranger to love.

It's getting late, who comes here with a mask over her face? Will she try the cards?

She does. She holds a coin in her palm so that I have to pick it out. Her skin is warm. I spread the cards. She chooses. The ten of diamonds. The three of clubs. Then the Queen of spades.

'A lucky card. The symbol of Venice. You win.'

She smiled at me and pulling away her mask revealed a pair of grey-green eyes with flecks of gold. Her cheekbones were high and rouged. Her hair, darker and redder than mine.

'Play again?'

She shook her head and had a waiter bring over a bottle of champagne. Not any champagne. Madame Clicquot. The only good thing to come out of France. She held the glass in a silent toast, perhaps to her own good fortune. The Queen of spades is a serious win and one we are usually careful to avoid. Still she did not speak, but watched me through the crystal and suddenly draining her glass stroked the side of my face. Only for a second she touched me and then she was gone and I was left with my heart smashing at my chest and three-quarters of a bottle of the best champagne. I was careful to conceal both.

I am pragmatic about love and have taken my pleasure with

both men and women, but I have never needed a guard for my heart. My heart is a reliable organ.

At midnight the gunpowder was triggered and the sky above St Mark's broke into a million coloured pieces. The fireworks lasted perhaps half an hour and during that time I was able to finger enough money to bribe a friend to take over my booth for a while. I slipped through the press towards the still bubbling glass slipper looking for her.

She had vanished. There were faces and dresses and masks and kisses to be had and a hand at every turn but she was not there. I was detained by an infantryman who held up two glass balls and asked if I would exchange them for mine. But I was in no mood for charming games and pushed past him, my eyes begging for a sign.

The roulette table. The gaming table. The fortune tellers. The fabulous three-breasted woman. The singing ape. The double-speed dominoes and the tarot.

She was not there.

She was nowhere.

My time was up and I went back to the booth of chance full of champagne and an empty heart.

'There was a woman looking for you,' said my friend. 'She left this.'

On the table was an earring. Roman by the look of it, curiously shaped, made of that distinct old yellow gold that these times do not know.

I put it in my ear and, spreading the cards in a perfect fan, took out the Queen of spades. No one else should win tonight. I would keep her card until she needed it.

Gaiety soon ages.

By three o'clock the revellers were drifting away through the arches around St Mark's or lying in piles by the cafés, opening early to provide strong coffee. The gaming was over. The Casino tellers were packing away their gaudy stripes and optimistic baize. I was off-duty and it was almost dawn. Usually, I go straight home and meet my stepfather on his way to the bakery. He slaps me about the shoulder and makes some joke about how much money I'm making. He's a curious man; a shrug of the shoulders and a wink and that's him. He's never thought it odd that his daughter cross-dresses for a living and sells second-hand purses on the side. But then, he's never thought it odd that his daughter was born with webbed feet.

'There are stranger things,' he said.

And I suppose there are.

This morning, there's no going home. I'm bolt upright, my legs are restless and the only sensible thing is to borrow a boat and calm myself in the Venetian way; on the water.

The Grand Canal is already busy with vegetable boats. I am the only one who seems intent on recreation and the others eye me curiously, in between steadying a load or arguing with a friend. These are my people, they can eye me as much as they wish.

I push on, under the Rialto, that strange half-bridge that can be drawn up to stop one half of this city warring with the other. They'll seal it eventually and we'll be brothers and mothers. But that will be the doom of paradox.

Bridges join but they also separate.

Out now, past the houses that lean into the water. Past the Casino itself. Past the money-lenders and the churches and the buildings of state. Out now into the lagoon with only the wind and the seagulls for company.

There is a certainty that comes with the oars, with the sense of generation after generation standing up like this and rowing like this with rhythm and ease. This city is littered with ghosts seeing to their own. No family would be complete without its ancestors.

Our ancestors. Our belonging. The future is foretold from the past and the future is only possible because of the past. Without past and future, the present is partial. All time is eternally present and so all time is ours. There is no sense in forgetting and every sense in dreaming. Thus the present is made rich. Thus the present is made whole. On the lagoon this morning, with the past at my elbow, rowing beside me, I see the future glittering on the water. I catch sight of myself in the water and see in the distortions of my face what I might become.

If I find her, how will my future be?

I will find her.

Somewhere between fear and sex passion is,

Passion is not so much an emotion as a destiny. What choice have I in the face of this wind but to put up sail and rest my oars?

Dawn breaks.

I spent the weeks that followed in a hectic stupor.

Is there such a thing? There is. It is the condition that most resembles a particular kind of mental disorder. I have seen ones like me in San Servelo. It manifests itself as a compulsion to be forever doing something, however meaningless. The body must move but the mind is blank.

I walked the streets, rowed circles around Venice, woke up in the middle of the night with my covers in impossible knots and my muscles rigid. I took to working double shifts at the Casino, dressing as a woman in the afternoon and a young man in the evenings. I ate when food was put in front of me and slept when my body was throbbing with exhaustion.

I lost weight.

I found myself staring into space, forgetting where I was going.

I was cold.

I never go to confession; God doesn't want us to confess, he wants us to challenge him, but for a while I went into our churches because they were built from the heart. Improbable hearts that I had never understood before. Hearts so full of longing that these old stones still cry out with their extasy. These are warm churches, built in the sun.

I sat at the back, listening to the music or mumbling through the service. I'm never tempted by God but I like his trappings. Not tempted but I begin to understand why others are. With this feeling inside, with this wild love that threatens, what safe places might there be? Where do you store gunpowder? How do you sleep at night again? If I were a little different I might turn passion into something holy and then I would sleep again. And then my extasy would be my extasy but I would not be afraid.

My flabby friend, who has decided I'm a woman, has asked me to marry him. He has promised to keep me in luxury and all kinds of fancy goods, provided I go on dressing as a young man in the comfort of our own home. He likes that. He says he'll get my moustaches and codpieces specially made and a rare old time we'll have of it, playing games and getting drunk. I was thinking of pulling a knife on him right there in the middle of the Casino, but my Venetian pragmatism stepped in and I thought I might have a little game myself. Anything now to relieve the ache of never finding her.

I've always wondered where his money comes from. Is it inherited? Does his mother still settle his bills?

No. He earns his money. He earns his money supplying the French army with meat and horses. Meat and horses he tells me that wouldn't normally feed a cat or mount a beggar.

How does he get away with it?

There's no one else who can supply so much so fast, anywhere; as soon as his orders arrive, the supplies are on their way.

It seems that Bonaparte wins his battles quickly or not at all. That's his way. He doesn't need quality, he needs action. He needs his men on their feet for a few days' march and a few days' battle. He needs horses for a single charge. That's enough. What does it matter if the horses are lame and the men are poisoned so long as they last so long as they're needed?

I'd be marrying a meat man.

I let him buy me champagne. Only the best. I hadn't tasted Madame Clicquot since the hot night in August. The rush of it along my tongue and into my throat brought back other memories. Memories of a single touch. How could anything so passing be so pervasive?

But Christ said, 'Follow me,' and it was done.

Sunk in these dreams, I hardly felt his hand along my leg, his fingers on my belly. Then I was reminded vividly of squid and their suckers and I shook him off shouting that I'd never marry him, not for all the Veuve Clicquot in France nor a Venice full of codpieces. His face was always red so it was hard to tell what he felt about these insults. He got up from where he'd been kneeling and straightened his waistcoat. He asked me if I wanted to keep my job.

'I'll keep my job because I'm good at it and clients like you come through the door every day.'

He hit me then. Not hard but I was shocked. I'd never been hit before. I hit him back. Hard.

He started to laugh and coming towards me squashed me flat against the wall. It was like being under a pile of fish. I didn't try to move, he was twice my weight at least and I'm no heroine. I'd nothing to lose either, having lost it already in happier times.

He left a stain on my shirt and threw a coin at me by way of goodbye.

What did I expect from a meat man?
I went back to the gaming floor.

November in Venice is the beginning of the catarrh season.
Catarrh is part of our heritage like St Mark's. Long ago, when
the Council of Three ruled in mysterious ways, any traitor or
hapless one done away with was usually announced to have died
of catarrh. In this way, no one was embarrassed. It's the fog that
rolls in from the lagoon and hides one end of the Piazza from
another that brings on our hateful congestion. It rains too,
mournfully and quietly, and the boatmen sit under sodden rags
and stare helplessly into the canals. Such weather drives away
the foreigners and that's the only good thing that can be said of
it. Even the brilliant water-gate at the Fenice turns grey.

On an afternoon when the Casino didn't want me and I didn't
want myself, I went to Florian's to drink and gaze at the Square.
It's a fulfilling pastime.

I had been sitting perhaps an hour when I had the feeling of
being watched. There was no one near me, but there was
someone behind a screen a little way off. I let my mind retreat
again. What did it matter? We are always watching or watched.
The waiter came over to me with a packet in his hand.

I opened it. It was an earring. It was the pair.

And she stood before me and I realised I was dressed as I
had been that night because I was waiting to work. My hand
went to my lip.

'You shaved it off,' she said.

I smiled. I couldn't speak.

She invited me to dine with her the following evening and I
took her address and accepted.

In the Casino that night I tried to decide what to do. She
thought I was a young man. I was not. Should I go to see her
as myself and joke about the mistake and leave gracefully? My
heart shrivelled at this thought. To lose her again so soon. And

what was myself? Was this breeches and boots self any less real than my garters? What was it about me that interested her?

You play, you win. You play, you lose. You play.

I was careful to steal enough to buy a bottle of the best champagne.

Lovers are not at their best when it matters. Mouths dry up, palms sweat, conversation flags and all the time the heart is threatening to fly from the body once and for all. Lovers have been known to have heart attacks. Lovers drink too much from nervousness and cannot perform. They eat too little and faint during their fervently wished consummation. They do not stroke the favoured cat and their face-paint comes loose. This is not all. Whatever you have set store by, your dress, your dinner, your poetry, will go wrong.

Her house was gracious, standing on a quiet waterway, fashionable but not vulgar. The drawing-room, enormous with great windows at either end and a fireplace that would have suited an idle wolfhound. It was simply furnished; an oval table and a *chaise-longue*. A few Chinese ornaments that she liked to collect when the ships came through. She had also a strange assortment of dead insects mounted in cases on the wall. I had never seen such things before and wondered about this enthusiasm.

She stood close to me as she took me through the house, pointing out certain pictures and books. Her hand guided my elbow at the stairs and when we sat down to eat she did not arrange us formally but put me beside her, the bottle in between.

We talked about the opera and the theatre and the visitors and the weather and ourselves. I told her that my real father had been a boatman and she laughed and asked could it be true that we had webbed feet?

'Of course,' I said and she laughed the more at this joke.

We had eaten. The bottle was empty. She said she had married late in life, had not expected to marry at all being stubborn and of independent means. Her husband dealt in rare books and manuscripts from the east. Ancient maps that showed the lairs of griffins and the haunts of whales. Treasure maps that claimed to know the whereabouts of the Holy Grail. He was a quiet and cultured man of whom she was fond.

He was away.

We had eaten, the bottle was empty. There was nothing more that could be said without strain or repetition. I had been with her more than five hours already and it was time to leave. As we stood up and she moved to get something I stretched out my arm, that was all, and she turned back into my arms so that my hands were on her shoulder blades and hers along my spine. We stayed thus for a few moments until I had courage enough to kiss her neck very lightly. She did not pull away. I grew bolder and kissed her mouth, biting a little at the lower lip.

She kissed me.

'I can't make love to you,' she said.

Relief and despair.

'But I can kiss you.'

And so, from the first, we separated our pleasure. She lay on the rug and I lay at right angles to her so that only our lips might meet. Kissing in this way is the strangest of distractions. The greedy body that clamours for satisfaction is forced to content itself with a single sensation and, just as the blind hear more acutely and the deaf can feel the grass grow, so the mouth becomes the focus of love and all things pass through it and are re-defined. It is a sweet and precise torture.

When I left her house some time later, I did not set off straight away, but watched her moving from room to room extinguishing the lights. Upwards she went, closing the dark behind her until there was only one light left and that was her own. She said she often read into the small hours while her husband was away.

Tonight she did not read. She paused briefly at the window and then the house was black.

What was she thinking?

What was she feeling?

I walked slowly through the silent squares and across the Rialto, where the mist was brooding above the water. The boats were covered and empty apart from the cats that make their homes under the seat boards. There was no one, not even the beggars who fold themselves and their rags into any doorway.

How is it that one day life is orderly and you are content, a little cynical perhaps but on the whole just so, and then without warning you find the solid floor is a trapdoor and you are now in another place whose geography is uncertain and whose customs are strange?

Travellers at least have a choice. Those who set sail know that things will not be the same as at home. Explorers are prepared. But for us, who travel along the blood vessels, who come to the cities of the interior by chance, there is no preparation. We who were fluent find life is a foreign language. Somewhere between the swamp and the mountains. Somewhere  between fear and sex. Somewhere between God and the Devil passion is and the way there is sudden and the way back is worse.

I'm surprised at myself talking in this way. I'm young, the world is before me, there will be others. I feel my first streak of defiance since I met her. My first upsurge of self. I won't see her again. I can go home, throw aside these clothes and move on. I can move out if I like. I'm sure the meat man can be persuaded to take me to Paris for a favour or two.

Passion, I spit on it.

I spat into the canal.

Then the moon came visible between the clouds, a full moon, and I thought of my mother rowing her way in faith to the terrible island.

The surface of the canal had the look of polished jet. I took off my boots slowly, pulling the laces loose and easing them free. Enfolded between each toe were my own moons. Pale and opaque. Unused. I had often played with them but I never thought they might be real. My mother wouldn't even tell me if the rumours were real and I have no boating cousins. My brothers are gone away.

Could I walk on that water?

Could I?

I faltered at the slippery steps leading into the dark. It was November, after all. I might die if I fell in. I tried balancing my foot on the surface and it dropped beneath into the cold nothingness.

Could a woman love a woman for more than a night?

I stepped out and in the morning they say a beggar was running round the Rialto talking about a young man who'd walked across the canal like it was solid.

I'm telling you stories. Trust me.

When we met again I had borrowed an officer's uniform. Or, more precisely, stolen it.

This is what happened.

At the Casino, well after midnight, a soldier had approached me and suggested an unusual wager. If I could beat him at billiards he would make me a present of his purse. He held it up before me. It was round and nicely padded and there must be some of my father's blood in me because I have never been able to resist a purse.

And if I lost? I was to make him a present of my purse. There was no mistaking his meaning.

We played, cheered on by a dozen bored gamblers and, to my surprise, the soldier played well. After a few hours at the Casino nobody plays anything well.

I lost.

We went to his room and he was a man who liked his women face down, arms outstretched like the crucified Christ. He was able and easy and soon fell asleep. He was also about my height. I left him his shirt and boots and took the rest.

She greeted me like an old friend and asked me straight away about the uniform.

'You're not a soldier.'

'It's fancy dress.'

I began to feel like Sarpi, that Venetian priest and diplomat, who said he never told a lie but didn't tell the truth to everyone. Many times that evening as we ate and drank and played dice I prepared to explain. But my tongue thickened and my heart rose up in self-defence.

'Feet,' she said.

'What?'

'Let me stroke your feet.'

Sweet Madonna, not my feet.

'I never take off my boots away from home. It's a nervous habit.'

'Then take off your shirt instead.'

Not my shirt, if I raised my shirt she'd find my breasts.

'In this inhospitable weather it would not be wise. Everyone has catarrh. Think of the fog.'

I saw her eyes stray lower. Did she expect my desire to be obvious?

What could I allow; my knees?

Instead I leaned forward and began to kiss her neck. She buried my head in her hair and I became her creature. Her smell, my atmosphere, and later when I was alone I cursed my nostrils for breathing the everyday air and emptying my body of her.

As I was leaving she said, 'My husband returns tomorrow.'

Oh.

As I was leaving she said, 'I don't know when I will see you again.'

Does she do this often? Does she walk the streets, when her husband goes away, looking for someone like me? Everyone in Venice has their weakness and their vice. Perhaps not only in Venice. Does she invite them to supper and hold them with her eyes and explain, a little sadly, that she can't make love? Perhaps this is her passion. Passion out of passion's obstacles. And me? Every game threatens a wild card. The unpredictable, the out of control. Even with a steady hand and a crystal ball we couldn't rule the world the way we wanted it. There are storms at sea and there are other storms inland. Only the convent windows look serenely out on both.

I went back to her house and banged on the door. She opened it a little. She looked surprised.

'I'm a woman,' I said, lifting up my shirt and risking the catarrh.

She smiled. 'I know.'

I didn't go home. I stayed.

The churches prepared for Christmas. Every Madonna was gilded and every Jesus re-painted. The priests took out their glorious golds and scarlets and the incense was especially sweet. I took to going to service twice a day to bask in the assurance of Our Lord. I've never had a conscience about basking. In summer I do it against the walls or I sit like the lizards of the Levant on top of our iron wells. I love the way wood holds heat, and if I can I take my boat and lie directly in the path of the sun for a day. My body loosens then, my mind floats away and I wonder if this is what holy men feel when they talk about their trances? I've seen holy men come from the eastern lands. We had an exhibit of them once to make up for the law prohibiting bull-baiting. Their bodies were loose but I have heard it's to do with the food they eat.

Basking can't be called holy, but if it achieves the same results will God mind? I don't think so. In the Old Testament the end always justified the means. We understand that in Venice, being a pragmatic people.

The sun is gone now and I must do my basking in other ways. Church basking is taking what's there and not paying for it. Taking the comfort and joy and ignoring the rest. Christmas but not Easter. I never bother with church at Easter. It's too gloomy, and besides the sun's out by then.

If I went to confession, what would I confess? That I cross-dress? So did Our Lord, so do the priests.

That I steal? So did Our Lord, so do the priests.

That I am in love?

The object of my love has gone away for Christmas. That's what they do at this time of year. He and she. I thought I'd mind, but since the first few days, when my stomach and chest were full of stones, I've been happy. Relieved almost. I've seen my old friends and walked by myself with almost the same sure-footedness that I used to. The relief comes from no more clandestine meetings. No more snatched hours. There was a particular week when she ate two breakfasts every day. One at home and one with me. One in the drawing-room and one in the Square. After that her lunches were a disaster.

She is much prone to going to the theatre, and because he does not enjoy the stage she goes alone. For a time she only saw one act of everything. In the interval she came to me.

Venice is full of urchins who will carry notes from one eager palm to another. In the hours we could not meet we sent messages of love and urgency. In the hours we could meet our passion was brief and fierce.

She dresses for me. I have never seen her in the same clothes twice.

Now, I am wholly given over to selfishness. I think about myself, I get up when I like, instead of at the crack of dawn just to watch her open the shutters. I flirt with waiters and gamblers and remember that I enjoy that. I sing to myself and I bask in churches. Is this freedom delicious because rare? Is any respite from love welcome because temporary? If she were gone for ever these days of mine would not be lit up. Is it because she will return that I take pleasure in being alone?

Hopeless heart that thrives on paradox; that longs for the beloved and is secretly relieved when the beloved is not there. That gnaws away at the night-time hours desperate for a sign and appears at breakfast so self-composed. That longs for certainty, fidelity, compassion, and plays roulette with anything precious.

Gambling is not a vice, it is an expression of our humanness. We gamble. Some do it at the gaming table, some do not. You play, you win, you play, you lose. You play.

The Holy child has been born. His mother is elevated. His father forgotten. The angels are singing in the choir stalls and God sits on the roof of each church and pours his blessing on to those below. What a wonder, joining yourself to God, pitting your wits against him, knowing that you win and lose simultaneously. Where else could you indulge without fear the exquisite masochism of the victim? Lie beneath his lances and close your eyes. Where else could you be so in control? Not in love, certainly.

His need for you is greater than your need for him because he knows the consequences of not possessing you, whereas you, who know nothing, can throw your cap in the air and live another day. You paddle in the water and he never crosses your mind, but he is busy recording the precise force of the flood around your ankles.

Bask in it. In spite of what the monks say, you can meet God without getting up early. You can meet God lounging in the pew. The hardship is a man-made device because man cannot exist without passion. Religion is somewhere between fear and sex. And God? Truly? In his own right, without our voices speaking for him? Obsessed I think, but not passionate.

In our dreams we sometimes struggle from the oceans of desire up Jacob's ladder to that orderly place. Then human voices wake us and we drown.

On New Year's Eve, a procession of boats alive with candles stretched down the Grand Canal. Rich and poor shared the same water and harboured the same dreams that next year, in its own way, would be better. My mother and father in their bakery best gave away loaves to the sick and the dispossessed. My father was drunk and had to be stopped from singing verses he had learnt in a French bordello.

Farther out, hidden away in the inner city, the exiles had their own observation. The dark canals were as dark as ever but a closer look revealed tattered satin on yellow bodies, the glint of a goblet from some subterranean hole. The slant-eyed children had stolen a goat and were solemnly slitting its throat when I rowed past. They stopped their red knives for a moment to watch me.

My philosopher friend was on her balcony. That is, a couple of crates fastened to the iron rings on either side of her nook. She was wearing something on her head, a circle, dark and heavy. I slid past her and she asked me what time it might be.

'Almost New Year.'

'I know it. It smells.'

She went back to dipping her cup into the canal and taking deep swigs. Only when I had gone on did I realise that her crown was made out of rats tied in a circle by their tails.

I saw no Jews. Their business is their own tonight.

It was bitterly cold. No wind but the icy air that freezes the lungs and bites at the lips. My fingers were numb about the oars and I almost thought of tying up my boat and hurrying to join the crowd pushing into St Mark's. But this was not a night for basking. Tonight the spirits of the dead are abroad speaking in tongues. Those who may listen will learn. She is at home tonight.

I rowed by her house, softly lit, and hoped to catch sight of her shadow, her arm, any sign. She was not visible, but I could imagine her seated, reading, a glass of wine by her side. Her husband would be in his study, poring over some new and fabulous treasure. The whereabouts of the Cross or the secret tunnels that lead to the centre of the earth where the fire dragons are.

I stopped by her water-gate, and climbing up the railing looked in through the window. She was alone. Not reading but staring at the palms of her hands. We had compared hands once, mine are very lined and hers, though they have been longer in this world, have the innocence of a child. What was she trying to see? Her future? Another year? Or was she trying to make sense of her past? To understand how the past had led to the present. Was she searching for the line of her desire for me?

I was about to tap on the window when her husband entered the room, startling her. He kissed her forehead and she smiled. I watched them together and saw more in a moment than I could have pondered in another year. They did not live in the fiery furnace she and I inhabited, but they had a calm and a way that put a knife to my heart.

I shivered with cold, suddenly realising that I was two storeys in mid-air. Even a lover is occasionally afraid.

The great clock in the Piazza struck a quarter to twelve. I hurried to my boat and rowed without feeling my hands or feet into the lagoon. In that stillness, in that quiet, I thought of my own future and what future there could be meeting in cafés and always dressing too soon. The heart is so easily mocked, believing that the sun can rise twice or that roses bloom because we want them to.

In this enchanted city all things seem possible. Time stops. Hearts beat. The laws of the real world are suspended. God sits in the rafters and makes fun of the Devil and the Devil pokes Our Lord with his tail. It has always been so. They say the boatmen have webbed feet and a beggar says he saw a young man walk on water.

If you should leave me, my heart will turn to water and flood away.

The Moors on the great clock swing back their hammers and strike in turn. Soon the Square will be a rush of bodies, their warm breath ascending and shaping little clouds above their heads. My breath shoots out straight in front of me like the fire dragon's. The ancestors cry from about the water and in St Mark's the organ begins. In between freezing and melting. In between love and despair. In between fear and sex, passion is. My oars lie flat on the water. It is New Year's Day, 1805.

· 3 ·

the Zero Winter

There's no such thing as a limited victory. Every victory leaves another resentment, another defeated and humiliated people. Another place to guard and defend and fear. What I learned about war in the years before I came to this lonely place were things any child could have told me.

'Will you kill people, Henri?'

'Not people, Louise, just the enemy.'

'What is enemy?'

'Someone who's not on your side.'

No one's on your side when you're the conqueror. Your enemies take up more room than your friends. Could so many straightforward ordinary lives suddenly become men to kill and women to rape? Austrians, Prussians, Italians, Spaniards, Egyptians, English, Poles, Russians. Those were the people who were either our enemies or our dependants. There were others, but the list is too long.

We never did invade England. We marched out of Boulogne leaving our little barges to rot and fought the Third Coalition instead. We fought at Ulm and Austerlitz. Eylau and Friedland. We fought on no rations, our boots fell apart, we slept two or three hours a night and died in thousands every day. Two years later Bonaparte was standing on a barge in the middle of a river hugging the Czar and saying we'd never have to fight again. *It was the English in our way and with Russia on our side the English would have to leave us alone.* No more coalitions, no more marches. Hot bread and the fields of France.

We believed him. We always did.

I lost an eye at Austerlitz. Domino was wounded and Patrick, who is still with us, never sees much past the next bottle. That should have been enough. I should have vanished the way soldiers do. Taken another name, set up shop in some small village, got married perhaps.

I didn't expect to come here. The view is good and the seagulls take bread from my window. One of the others here boils seagulls, but only in the winter. In summer they're full of worms.
Winter.
The unimaginable zero winter.

'We march on Moscow,' he said when the Czar betrayed him. It was not his intention, he wanted a speedy campaign. A blow to Russia for daring to set herself against him again. He thought he could always win battles the way he had always won battles. Like a circus dog he thought every audience would marvel at his tricks, but the audience was getting used to him. The Russians didn't even bother to fight the Grande Armée in any serious way, they kept on marching, burning villages behind them, leaving nothing to eat, nowhere to sleep. They marched into winter and we followed them. Into the Russian winter in our summer overcoats. Into the snow in our glued-together boots. When our horses died of the cold we slit their bellies and slept with our feet inside the guts. One man's horse froze around him; in the morning when he tried to take his feet out they were stuck, entombed in the brittle entrails. We couldn't free him, we had to leave him. He wouldn't stop screaming.

Bonaparte travelled by sledge, sending desperate orders down the lines, trying to make us outmanœuvre the Russians in just one place. We couldn't outmanœuvre them. We could hardly walk.

The consequences of burning the villages were not only our consequences; they were those of the people who lived there. Peasants whose lives ran with the sun and moon. Like my mother and father, they accepted each season and looked forward to the harvest. They worked hard in the hours of daylight and comforted themselves with stories from the Bible and stories of the forest. Their forests were full of spirits, some good some not, but every family had a happy story to tell; how their child was saved or their only cow brought back to life by the agency of a spirit.

They called the Czar 'the Little Father', and they worshipped him as they worshipped God. In their simplicity I saw a mirror of my own longing and understood for the first time my own need for a little father that had led me this far. They are a hearth people, content to bolt the door at night and eat thick soup and black bread. They sing songs to ward the night away and, like us, they take their animals into the kitchen in winter. In winter the cold is too much to endure and the ground is harder than a soldier's blade. They can only light the lamps and live on the food in the cellar and dream of the spring.

When the army burned their villages, the people helped to set fire to their own homes, to their years of work and common sense. They did it for the little father. They turned themselves out into the zero winter and went to their deaths in ones and twos or in families. They walked to the woods and sat by the frozen rivers, not for long, the blood soon chills, but long enough for some of them to be still singing songs as we passed by. Their voices were caught in the fierce air and carried through the stubble of their houses to us.

We had killed them all without firing a shot. I prayed for the snow to fall and bury them for ever. When the snow falls you can almost believe the world is clean again.

Is every snowflake different? No one knows.

I have to stop writing now. I have to take my exercise. They expect you to take your exercise at the same time each day, otherwise they start to worry about your health. They like to keep us healthy here so that when the visitors come they go away satisfied. I hope I will have a visitor today.

Watching my comrades die was not the worst thing about that war, it was watching them live. I had heard stories about the human body and the human mind, the conditions it can adapt to, the ways it chooses to survive. I had heard tales of people who were burnt in the sun and grew another skin, thick and black like the top of overcooked porridge. Others who learned not to sleep so that they wouldn't be eaten by wild animals. The body clings to life at any cost. It even eats itself. When there's no food it turns cannibal and devours its fat, then its muscle then its bones. I've seen soldiers, mad with hunger and cold, chop off their own arms and cook them. How long could you go on chopping? Both arms. Both legs. Ears. Slices from the trunk. You could chop yourself down to the very end and leave the heart to beat in its ransacked palace.

No. Take the heart first. Then you don't feel the cold so much. The pain so much. With the heart gone, there's no reason to stay your hand. Your eyes can look on death and not tremble. It's the heart that betrays us, makes us weep, makes us bury our friends when we should be marching ahead. It's the heart that sickens us at night and makes us hate who we are. It's the heart that sings old songs and brings memories of warm days and makes us waver at another mile, another smouldering village.

To survive the zero winter and that war we made a pyre of our hearts and put them aside for ever. There's no pawnshop for the heart. You can't take it in and leave it awhile in a clean cloth and redeem it in better times.

You can't make sense of your passion for life in the face of death, you can only give up your passion. Only then can you begin to survive.

And if you refuse?

If you felt for every man you murdered, every life you broke in two, every slow and painful harvest you destroyed, every child whose future you stole, madness would throw her noose around your neck and lead you into the dark woods where the rivers are polluted and the birds are silent.

When I say I lived with heartless men, I use the word correctly.

As the weeks wore on, we talked about going home and home stopped being a place where we quarrel as well as love. It stopped being a place where the fire goes out and there is usually some unpleasant job to be done. Home became the focus of joy and sense. We began to believe that we were fighting this war so that we could go home. To keep home safe, to keep home as we started to imagine it. Now that our hearts were gone there was no reliable organ to stem the steady tide of sentiment that stuck to our bayonets and fed our damp fires. There was nothing we wouldn't believe to get us through: God was on our side, the Russians were devils. Our wives depended on this war. France depended on this war. There was no alternative to this war.

And the heaviest lie? That we could go home and pick up where we had left off. That our hearts would be waiting behind the door with the dog.

Not all men are as fortunate as Ulysses.

Our sustaining hope as the temperatures dropped and we gave up speech was to reach Moscow. A great city where there would be food and fire and friends. Bonaparte was confident of peace once we had dealt a decisive blow. He was already writing surrender notices, filling the space with humiliation and leaving just enough room at the bottom for the Czar to sign. He seemed to think we were winning when all we were doing was running behind. But he had furs to keep his blood optimistic.

Moscow is a city of domes, built to be beautiful, a city of squares and worship. I did see it, briefly. The gold domes lit yellow and orange and the people gone.

They set fire to it. Even when Bonaparte arrived, days ahead of the rest of the army, it was blazing and it went on blazing. It was a difficult city to burn.

We camped away from the flames and I served him that night on a scrawny chicken surrounded by parsley the cook cherishes in a dead man's helmet. I think it was that night that I knew I couldn't stay any longer. I think it was that night that I started to hate him.

I didn't know what hate felt like, not the hate that comes after love. It's huge and desperate and it longs to be proved wrong. And every day it's proved right it grows a little more monstrous. If the love was passion, the hate will be obsession. A need to see the once-loved weak and cowed and beneath pity. Disgust is close and dignity is far away. The hate is not only for the once loved, it's for yourself too; how could you ever have loved this?

When Patrick arrived some days later I searched for him in the blistering cold and found him wrapped in sacks with a jar of some colourless liquid beside him. He was still look-out, this time watching for surprise enemy movements, but he was never sober and not all of his sightings were taken seriously. He waved the jar at me and said he'd got it in exchange for a life. A peasant had begged to be allowed to die with his family in the honourable way, in the cold all together, and had offered Patrick the jar. Whatever was in it had put him in a gloomy temper. I smelled it. It smelt of age and hay. I started to cry and my tears fell like diamonds.

Patrick picked one up and told me not to waste my salt.

Meditatively, he ate it.

'It goes well with this spirit it does.'

There is a story about an exiled Princess whose tears turned to jewels as she walked. A magpie followed her and picked up all the jewels and dropped them on the windowsill of a thoughtful Prince. This Prince scoured the land until he found the Princess and they lived happily ever after. The magpie was made a royal bird and given an oak forest to live in and the Princess had her tears made into a great necklace, not to wear, but to look at whenever she felt unhappy. When she looked at the necklace, she knew that she was not.

'Patrick, I'm going to desert. Will you come with me?'

He laughed. 'I may only be half alive now, but sure as I know I'd be fully dead if I set out with you in this wilderness.'

I didn't try to persuade him. We sat together sharing the sacks and the spirit and dreamed separately.

Would Domino come?

He didn't speak much since his injury, which had blown away one side of his face. He wore a cloth wrapped round his head and overlapping his scars to mop up the bleeding. If he stayed out in the cold for too long the scars opened and filled his mouth with blood and pus. The doctor explained it to him; something about the wounds going septic after he'd had himself stitched up. The doctor shrugged. It was a battle, he'd done what he could but what could he do with arms and legs everywhere and nothing but grape brandy to ease the pain and still the wounds? Too many soldiers are wounded, it would be better if they died. Domino was hunched up in Bonaparte's sledge in the rough tent where it was kept and he slept. He was lucky, looking after Bonaparte's equipment just as I was lucky working in the officers' kitchen. We were both warmer and better fed than anyone else. That makes it sound cosy ...

We avoided the worst ravages of frostbite and we got food every day. But canvas and potatoes do not challenge the zero winter; if anything, they denied us the happy oblivion that comes with dying of cold. When soldiers finally lie down, knowing they won't get up again, most of them smile. There's a comfort in falling asleep in the snow.

He looked ill.

'I'm going to desert, Domino. Will you come with me?'

He couldn't talk at all that day, the pain was too bad, but he wrote in the snow that had drifted still soft under the tent.

CRAZY.

'I'm not crazy, Domino, you've been laughing at me since I joined up. Eight years you've been laughing at me. Take me seriously.'

He wrote, WHY?

'Because I can't stay here. These wars will never end. Even if we get home, there'll be another war. I thought he'd end wars for ever, that's what he said. One more, he said, one more and then there'll be peace and it's always been one more. I want to stop now.'

He wrote, FUTURE. And then he put a line through it.

What did he mean? His future? My future? I thought back to those sea-salt days when the sun had turned the grass yellow and men had married mermaids. I started my little book then, the one I still have and Domino had turned on me and called the future a dream. *There's only the present, Henri.*

He had never talked of what he wanted to do, where he was going, he never joined in the aimless conversations that clustered round the idea of something better in another time. He didn't believe in the future, only the present, and as our future, our years, had turned so relentlessly into identical presents, I understood him more. Eight years had passed and I was still at war, cooking chickens, waiting to go home for good. Eight years of talking about the future and seeing it turn into the present. Years of thinking, 'In another year, I'll be doing something different,' and in another year doing just the same.

Future. Crossed out.

That's what war does.

I don't want to worship him any more. I want to make my own mistakes. I want to die in my own time.

Domino was looking at me. The snow had already covered his words.

He wrote, YOU GO.

He tried to smile. His mouth couldn't smile but his eyes were bright, and jumping up in the old way, in the way he'd jumped to pick apples from the tallest trees, he snatched an icicle from the blackened canvas and handed it to me.

It was beautiful. Formed from the cold and glittering in the centre. I looked again. There was something inside it, running through the middle from top to bottom. It was a piece of thin gold that Domino usually wore round his neck. He called it his talisman. What had he done with it and why was he giving it to me?

Making signs with his hands he made me understand that he could no longer wear it around his neck because of his sores. He had cleaned it and hung it out of sight and this morning had seen it so encased.

An ordinary miracle.

I tried to give it back, but he pushed me away until I nodded and said I'd hang it on my belt when I left.

I think I had known he wouldn't come. He wouldn't leave the horses. They were the present.

When I got back to the kitchen tent, Patrick was waiting for me with a woman I had never met. She was a *vivandière*. Only a handful were left and they were strictly for the officers. The pair of them were wolfing chicken legs and offered one to me.

'Rest your heart,' said Patrick, seeing my horror, 'these don't belong to Our Lord, our friend here came by them and when I came looking for you, she was already in here doing a bit of cooking.'

'Where did you get them?'

'I fucked for them, the Russians have got plenty and there's still plenty of Russians in Moscow.'

I blushed and mumbled something about the Russians having fled.

She laughed and said the Russians could hide under the snowflakes. Then she said, 'They're all different.'

'What?'

'Snowflakes. Think of that.'

I did think of that and I fell in love with her.

When I said I was leaving that night she asked if she could come with me.

'I can help you.'

I would have taken her with me even if she'd been lame.

'If you're both going,' said Patrick, draining the last of his evil spirit, 'I'll come along too. I don't fancy it here on my own.'

I was taken aback and for a moment consumed with jealousy. Perhaps Patrick loved her? Perhaps she loved him?

Love. In the middle of a zero winter. What was I thinking?

We packed the rest of her food and a good deal of Bonaparte's. He trusted me and I had never given him reason not to.

Well, even great men can be surprised.

We took what there was and she returned wrapped in a huge fur, another of her souvenirs of Moscow. As we set off, I slipped into Domino's tent and left him as much of the food as I dared spare and scrawled my name in the ice on the sledge.

Then we were gone.

We walked for a night and a day without stopping. Our legs assumed an ungainly rhythm and we were afraid to stop in case our lungs or our legs buckled under us. We didn't talk, we wrapped our noses and mouths as tightly as we could and let our eyes poke out like slits. There was no fresh snow. The hard ground rang at our heels.

I remembered a woman with her baby, her heels sparking the cobbles.

'Happy New Year, soldier.'

Why do all happy memories feel like yesterday though years have passed?

We were heading in the direction we had come, using the charred villages as gruesome signposts, but our progress was slow and we were afraid to stick directly to the roads for fear of Russian troops or some of our own army, greedy and desperate. Mutineers, or traitors as they were more usually called, found no leniency and were given no opportunity to make their excuses. We camped where we could find some natural shelter and huddled together for warmth. I wanted to touch her, but her body was covered all over and my hands were gloved.

On the seventh night, coming out of the forest, we found a hut full of primitive muskets, a dump for the Russian troops we supposed, but there was no one. We were weary and took our chance in there, using dregs of gunpowder from the barrels to light a fire. It was the first night we had had enough shelter to take off our boots and Patrick and I were soon stretching our toes at the blaze, risking permanent damage to our feet.

Our companion loosed her laces but kept her boots on, and seeing my surprise at forgoing this unexpected luxury said, 'My father was a boatman. Boatmen do not take off their boots.' We were silent, either out of respect for her customs or sheer exhaustion, but it was she who offered to tell us her story if we chose to listen.

'A fire and a tale,' said Patrick. 'Now all we need is a drop of something hot,' and he fathomed from the bottom of his unfathomable pockets another stoppered jar of evil spirit.

This was her story.

I have always been a gambler. It's a skill that comes naturally to me like thieving and loving. What I didn't know by instinct I picked up from working the Casino, from watching others play and learning what it is that people value and therefore what it is they will risk. I learned how to put a challenge in such a way as to make it irresistible. We gamble with the hope of winning, but it's the thought of what we might lose that excites us.

How you play is a temperamental thing; cards, dice, dominoes, jacks, such preferences are frills merely. All gamblers sweat. I come from the city of chances, where everything is possible but where everything has a price. In this city great fortunes are won and lost overnight. It has always been so. Ships that carry silk and spices sink, the servant betrays the master, the secret is out and the bell tolls another accidental death. But penniless adventurers have always been welcome here too, they are good luck and very often their good luck rubs off on themselves. Some who come on foot leave on horseback and others who trumpeted their estate beg on the Rialto. It has always been so.

The astute gambler always keeps something back, something to play with another time; a pocket watch, a hunting dog. But the Devil's gambler keeps back something precious, something to gamble with only once in a lifetime. Behind the secret panel he keeps it, the valuable, fabulous thing that no one suspects he has.

I knew a man like that; not a drunkard sniffing after every wager nor an addict stripping the clothes off his back rather than go home. A thoughtful man who they say had trade with gold and death. He lost heavily, as gamblers do; he won surprisingly, as gamblers do, but he never showed much emotion, never led me to suspect that much important was at stake. A hobbyist, I thought, dismissing him. You see, I like passion, I like to be among the desperate.

I was wrong to dismiss him. He was waiting for the wager that would seduce him into risking what he valued. He was a true gambler, he was prepared to risk the valuable, fabulous thing but not for a dog or a cock or the casual dice.

On a quiet evening, when the tables were half empty and the domino sets lay in their boxes, he was there, wandering, fluttering, drinking and flirting.

I was bored.

Then a man came into the room, not one of our regulars, not one any of us knew, and after a few half-hearted games of chance he spied this figure and engaged him in conversation. They talked for upwards of half an hour and so intently that we thought they must be old friends and lost our curiosity in the assumption of habit. But the rich man with his strangely bowed companion by his side asked leave to make an announcement, a most remarkable wager, and we cleared the central floor and let him speak.

It seemed that his companion, this stranger, had come from the wastes of the Levant, where exotic lizards breed and all is unusual. In his country, no man bothered with paltry fortunes at the gaming table, they played for higher stakes.

A life.

The wager was a life. The winner should take the life of the loser in whatsoever way he chose. However slowly he chose, with whatever instruments he chose. What was certain was that only one life would be spared.

Our rich friend was clearly excited. His eyes looked past the faces and tables of the gaming room into a space we could not inhabit; into the space of pain and loss. What could it matter to him that he might lose fortunes?

He had fortunes to lose.

What could it matter to him that he might lose mistresses?

There are women enough.

What would it matter to him that he might lose his life?

He had one life. He cherished it.

There were those that night who begged him not to go on with it, who saw a sinister aspect in this unknown old man, who were perhaps afraid of being made the same offer and of refusing.

What you risk reveals what you value.

These were the terms.

A game of three.

The first, the roulette, where only fate is queen.

The second, the cards, where skill has some part.

The third, the dominoes, where skill is paramount and chance is there in disguise.

Will she wear your colours?

This is the city of disguises.

The terms were agreed and strictly supervised. The winner was two out of three or in the event of some onlooker crying Nay! a tie, chosen at random, by the manager of the Casino.

The terms seemed fair. More than fair in this cheating world, but there were still some who felt uneasy about the unknown man, unassuming and unthreatening as he seemed.

If the Devil plays dice, will he come like this?

Will he come so quietly and whisper in our ear?

If he came as an angel of light, we should be immediately on our guard.

The word was given: Play on.

We drank throughout the first game, watching the red and black spin under our hands, watching the bright streak of metal dally with one number, then another, innocent of win or lose. At first it seemed as though our rich friend must win, but at the last moment the ball sprang out of its slot and spun again with that dwindling sickening sound that marks the last possible change.

The wheel came to rest.

It was the stranger whom fortune loved.

There was a moment's silence, we expected some sign, some worry on one part, some satisfaction on another, but with faces of wax, the two men got up and walked to the optimistic baize. The cards. No man knows what they may hold. A man must trust his hand.

Swift dealing. These were accustomed to the game.

They played for perhaps an hour and we drank. Drank to keep our lips wet, our lips that dried every time a card fell and the stranger seemed doomed to victory. There was an odd sense in the room that the stranger must not win, that for all our sakes he must lose. We willed our rich friend to weld his wits with his luck and he did.

At the cards, he won and they were even.

The two men met each other's gaze for a moment before they seated themselves in front of the dominoes and in each face was something of the other. Our rich friend had assumed a more calculating expression, while his challenger's face was more thoughtful, less wolfish than before.

It was clear from the start that they were evenly matched at this game too. They played deftly, judging the gaps and the numbers, making lightning calculations, baffling each other. We had stopped drinking. There was neither sound nor movement save the clicking of the dominoes on the marble table.

It was past midnight. I heard the water lapping at the stones below. I heard my saliva in my throat. I heard the dominoes clicking on the marble table.

There were no dominoes left. No gaps.

The stranger had won.

The two men stood up simultaneously, shook hands. Then the rich man placed his hands on the marble, and we saw they were shaking. Fine comfortable hands that were shaking. The stranger noticed and with a little smile suggested they complete the terms of their wager.

None of us spoke up, none of us tried to stop him. Did we want it to happen? Did we hope that one life might substitute for many?

I do not know our motives, I only know that we were silent.

This was the death: dismemberment piece by piece beginning with the hands.

The rich man nodded almost imperceptibly and, bowing to

us, left in the company of the stranger. We heard nothing more, never saw either of them again, but one day, months later, when we had comforted ourselves that it was a joke, that they had parted at the corner, out of sight, given each other a fright, nothing more, we received a pair of hands, manicured and quite white, mounted on green baize in a glass case. Between the finger and thumb of the left was a roulette ball and between the finger and thumb of the right, a domino.

The manager hung the case on the wall and there it hangs today.

I have said that behind the secret panel lies a valuable, fabulous thing. We are not always conscious of it, not always aware of what it is we hide from prying eyes or that those prying eyes may sometimes be our own.

There was a night, eight years ago, when a hand that took me by surprise slid the secret panel and showed me what it was I kept to myself.

My heart is a reliable organ, how could it be my heart? My everyday, work-hard heart that laughed at life and gave nothing away. I have seen dolls from the east that fold in one upon the other, the one concealing the other and so I know that the heart may conceal itself.

It was a game of chance I entered into and my heart was the wager. Such games can only be played once.

Such games are better not played at all.

It was a woman I loved and you will admit that is not the usual thing. I knew her for only five months. We had nine nights together and I never saw her again. You will admit that is not the usual thing.

I have always preferred the cards to the dice so it should have come as no surprise to me to have drawn a wild card.

The Queen of spades.

She lived simply and elegantly and her husband was sometimes called away to examine a new rarity (he dealt in books and maps); he was called away soon after we met. For nine days and nights we stayed in her house, never opening the door, never looking out of the window.

We were naked and not ashamed.

And we were happy.

On the ninth day I was left alone for a while because she had certain household affairs to attend to before her husband's return. On that day the rain splashed against the windows and filled up the canals below, churning the rubbish that lies under the surface, the rubbish that feeds the rats and the exiles in their dark mazes. It was early in the New Year. She had told me she loved me. I never doubted her word because I could feel how true it was. When she touched me I knew I was loved and with a passion I had not felt before. Not in another and not in myself.

Love is a fashion these days and in this fashionable city we know how to make light of love and how to keep our hearts at bay. I thought of myself as a civilised woman and I found I was a savage. When I thought of losing her I wanted to drown both of us in some lonely place rather than feel myself a beast that has no friend.

On the ninth night we ate and drank as usual alone in the house, the servants dismissed. She liked to cook omelettes with herbs and these we ate with hot radishes she had got from a merchant. Occasionally our conversation faltered and I saw tomorrow in her eyes. Tomorrow when we would part and resume our life of strange meetings in unfamiliar quarters. There was a café we usually went to, full of students from Padua and artists seeking inspiration. She was not known there. Her friends could not find her out. Thus we had met and met too in hours that did not belong to us, until this gift of nine nights.

I did not meet her sadness; it was too heavy.

There is no sense in loving someone you can never wake up to except by chance. J.F.

The gambler is led on in the hope of a win, thrilled with the fear of losing and when he wins he believes his luck is there, that he will win again.

If nine nights were possible why not ten?

So it goes and the weeks pass waiting for the tenth night, waiting to win again and all the time losing bit by bit that valuable fabulous thing that cannot be replaced.

Her husband dealt only in what was unique, he never bought a treasure someone else might have.

Would he buy my heart then and give it to her?

I had already wagered it for nine nights. In the morning when I left I did not say I would not see her again. I simply made no arrangement. She did not press me to do so, she had often said that as she got older she took what she could of life but expected little.

Then I was gone.

Every time I was tempted to go to her I went to the Casino instead and watched some fool humiliating himself at the tables. I could gamble on another night, reduce myself a little more, but after the tenth night would come the eleventh and the twelfth and so on into the silent space that is the pain of never having enough. The silent space full of starving children. She loved her husband.

I decided to marry.

There was a man who had wanted me for some time, a man I had refused, cursed. A man I despised. A rich man with fat fingers. He liked me to dress as a boy. I like to dress as a boy now and then. We had that in common.

He came to the Casino every night, playing for high stakes but not gambling with anything too precious. He was no fool. He clasped me with his terrible hands, with fingertips that had the feel of boils bursting, and asked me if I'd changed my mind about his offer. We could travel the world he said. Just the three of us. Him, me and my codpiece.

The city I come from is a changeable city. It is not always the same size. Streets appear and disappear overnight, new waterways force themselves over dry land. There are days when you cannot walk from one end to the other, so far is the journey, and there are days when a stroll will take you round your kingdom like a tin-pot Prince.

I had begun to feel that this city contained only two people who sensed each other and never met. Whenever I went out I hoped and dreaded to see the other. In the faces of strangers I saw one face and in the mirror I saw my own.

The world.

The world is surely wide enough to walk without fear.

We were married without ceremony and set off straight away to France, to Spain, to Constantinople even. He was as good as his word in that respect and I drank my coffee in a different place each month.

There was, in a certain city where the climate was fine, a young Jewish man who loved to drink his coffee at the pavement cafés and watch the world go by. He saw sailors and travellers and women with swans in their hair and all manner of fanciful distractions.

One day he saw a young woman flying past, her clothes flying out behind her.

She was beautiful and because he knew that beauty makes us good he asked her to stop awhile and share his coffee.

'I'm running away,' she said.

'Who are you running away from?'

'Myself.'

But she agreed to sit awhile because she was lonely.

His name was Salvadore.

They talked about the mountain ranges and the opera. They talked about animals with metal coats that can swim the length of a river without coming up for air. They talked about the valuable, fabulous thing that everyone has and keeps a secret. 'Here,' said Salvadore, 'look at this,' and he took out a box enamelled on the outside and softly lined on the inside and on the inside was his heart.

'Give me yours in exchange.'

But she couldn't because she was not travelling with her heart, it was beating in another place.

She thanked the young man and went back to her husband, whose hands crept over her body like crabs.

And the young man thought often of a beautiful woman on that sunny day when the wind had pushed out her earrings like fins.

We travelled for two years, then I stole his watch and what money he had on him and left him. I dressed as a boy to escape detection, and while he snored off his red wine and most of a goose I lost myself in the dark that has always been a friend.

I got odd jobs on ships and in grand houses, learned to speak five languages and did not see that city of destiny for another three years, then I caught a ship home on a whim and because I wanted my heart back. I should have known better than to risk my luck in the shrinking city. He soon found me out and his fury at being robbed and abandoned had not abated, even though he was living with another woman by then.

A friend of his, a sophisticated man, suggested a little wager for the two of us, a way of solving our differences. We were to play cards and if I won, I should have my freedom to come and go as I pleased and enough money to do so. If I lost, my husband should do with me as he pleased, though he was not to molest or murder me.

What choice had I?

At the time, I thought I played badly, but I later discovered by chance that the pack was fixed, that the wager had been fixed from the start. As I told you, my husband is no fool.

It was the Jack of hearts that caught me out.

When I lost, I thought he would force me home and that would be an end to it, but instead he kept me waiting three days and then sent a message for me to meet him.

He was with his friend when I arrived and an officer of high rank, a Frenchman whom I discovered to be General Murat.

This officer looked me up and down in my woman's clothes then asked me to change into my easy disguise. He was all admiration and, turning from me, withdrew a large bag from within his effects and placed it on the table between himself and my husband.

'This is the price we agreed then,' he said.

And my husband, his fingers trembling, counted it out.

He had sold me.

I was to join the army, to join the Generals for their pleasure.

It was, Murat assured me, quite an honour.

They didn't give me enough time to collect my heart, only my luggage, but I'm grateful to them for that; this is no place for a heart.

She was silent. Patrick and I, who had not uttered a word nor moved at all save to shield our scorching feet, felt unable to speak. It was she who broke the silence again.

'Pass me that evil spirit, a story deserves a reward.'

She seemed carefree and the shadows that had crossed her face throughout her story had lifted, but I felt my own just beginning.

She would never love me.

I had found her too late.

I wanted to ask her more about her watery city that is never the same, to see her eyes light up for love of something if not for love of me, but she was already spreading her furs and settling to sleep. Cautiously, I put my hand to her face and she smiled, reading my thoughts.

'When we get through this snow, I'll take you to the city of disguises and you'll find one that suits you.'

Another one. I'm already in disguise in these soldiers' clothes. I want to go home.

During the night, while we slept, the snows began again. We couldn't push open the door in the morning, not Patrick nor I nor the three of us together. We had to break down the wood where it had splintered and because I am still skinny, I was the one bundled face first into a snowdrift banked taller than a man.

With my hands I began scooping away that deadly heady stuff that tempts me to plunge in and never bother to come out. Snow doesn't look cold, it doesn't look as though it has any temperature at all. And when it falls and you catch those pieces of nothing in your hands, it seems so unlikely that they could hurt anyone. Seems so unlikely that simple multiplication can make such a difference.

Perhaps not. Even Bonaparte was beginning to learn that numbers count. In this vast country there are miles and men and snowflakes beyond our resources.

I took off my gloves to keep them dry and watched my hands alter from red to white to beautiful sea blue where the veins rear up almost purple, almost the colour of anemones. I could feel my lungs beginning to freeze.

At home, on the farm, the frost at midnight brightens the ground and hardens the stars. The cold there slashes you like a whip, but it is never so cold that you feel yourself freezing from the inside. That the air you breathe is seizing the fluids and mists and turning them into lakes of ice. When I drew breath I felt as though I were being embalmed.

It took me most of the morning to clear away the snow enough to open the door. We left with gunpowder and very little food and tried to go on tracing our way towards Poland, or the Duchy of Warsaw as Napoleon had designated it. Our plan was to skirt along the borders, then down through Austria, across the

Danube, heading for Venice or Trieste if the ports were blocked. A journey of some 1,300 miles.

Villanelle was skilful with the compass and map; she said it was one of the advantages of sleeping with Generals.

Progress was slower than usual for us thanks to the snowdrifts, and we might have died less than two weeks after we'd set out if it hadn't been for a detour we were forced to make that led us to a cluster of houses away from the spread of our armies. When we saw the smoke rising in the distance we thought it was another desolate sacrifice, but Patrick swore he could see rooftops, not shells, and we had to trust that it was not the evil spirit guiding us. If it was a burning village, troops would be close at hand.

On Villanelle's advice, we pretended to be Poles. She spoke the language as well as Russian, and explained to the suspicious villagers that we had been captured by the French for service but had murdered our guards and escaped. Hence the uniforms, stolen to avoid detection. When the Russian peasants heard we had murdered some Frenchmen, their faces were alive with joy, and they hurried us indoors with promises of food and shelter. From them, through Villanelle's interpretation, we learned how little of the country had been spared, how comprehensive had been the burnings. Their own homes had escaped because they were sufficiently remote and mainly because a Russian high ranker was in love with the daughter of the goatherd. An odd story of a chance seduction that had excited his heart as well as his imagination. This Russian had promised to spare the village and re-routed his troops accordingly, so that when we French followed we too had gone another way.

Love it seems can survive even a war and a zero winter. Like the snow-raspberries, our host explained, love is like that, and he told us how these flimsy delicacies appear always in February, whatever the weather, whatever the prospects. No one knows why, when pines are withered at the roots and rough sheep have to be kept indoors, these impossible hot-house things still grow.

The goatherd's daughter was something of a celebrity.

Villanelle had pretended she and I were married and we were put to sleep in the same bed, while poor Patrick had to share with their son, who was an amiable idiot. On the second morning we heard cries coming from Patrick's loft and found him pinned on his back by the son, who was the size of an ox. This boy had a wooden flute and was playing tunes of a kind while Patrick groaned beneath. We couldn't move him and it was only our host's wife who, giving him a flick with her cloth, sent the boy roaring and weeping out into the snow. A little later, he crept in and lay at his mother's feet, his eyes wide open, staring.

'He's a good boy,' she told Villanelle.

It seemed he had been visited by a spirit at birth and this spirit had offered him brains or strength. Our host's wife shrugged. What good were brains in this place with the sheep and goats to care for and the trees to fell? They had thanked the spirit and asked for strength, and now their son, who was only fourteen, could carry five men or lift a cow across his shoulders like a lamb. He ate from a bucket because there was no dish large enough to comfort his appetite. And so at meals the three of us sat with our bowls and the peasant and his wife with their hard bread and, at the end of the table, their son with his shoulders blocking the window and his ladle dipping in and out of his bucket.

'Will he marry?' Villanelle asked.

'Yes indeed,' said our host, looking surprised. 'Any woman would want such a fine strong man for her husband. We will find someone for him in time.'

At night I lay awake next to Villanelle and listened to her breathing. She slept curled up with her back towards me and never made any sign that she wanted to be touched. I touched her when I was sure she was asleep. Ran my hand up her spine and wondered if all women felt so soft and so firm. One night she turned over suddenly and told me to make love to her.

'I don't know how.'

'Then I'll make love to you.'

When I think of that night, here in this place where I will always be, my hands tremble and my muscles ache. I lose all sense of day or night, I lose all sense of my work, writing this story, trying to convey to you what really happened. Trying not to make up too much. I can think of it by mistake, my eyes blurring the words in front of me, my pen lifting and staying lifted, I can think of it for hours and yet it is always the same moment I think of. Her hair as she bent over me, red with streaks of gold, her hair on my face and chest and looking up at her through her hair. She let it fall over me and I felt I was lying in the long grass, safe.

When we left the village we left with a series of short cuts drawn for us on our map and more food than they should have spared. I felt guilty because apart from Villanelle, they should have killed us.

Wherever we went we found men and women who hated the French. Men and women whose futures had been decided for them. They were not articulate thinking people, they were people of the land who were content with little and zealous in their worship of custom and God. Although their lives were not much changed, they felt slighted because their leaders had been slighted, they felt out of control and resented the armies and the puppet Kings Bonaparte left behind. Bonaparte always claimed he knew what was good for a people, knew how to improve, how to educate. He did; he improved wherever he went, but he always forgot that even simple people want the freedom to make their own mistakes.

Bonaparte wanted no mistakes.

In Poland we pretended we were all Italian and received

the sympathy due to one occupied race from another. When Villanelle revealed her Venetian origins, hands flew across mouths and saintly women crossed themselves. Venice, the city of Satan. Was it really like that? and even the most disapproving crept up to her and asked whether or not there were truly 11,000 prostitutes all richer than Kings?

Villanelle, who loved to tell stories, wove for their wildest dreams. She even said that the boatmen had webbed feet, and while Patrick and I could hardly swallow our laughter, the Poles grew wide-eyed and one even risked excommunication by suggesting that perhaps Christ had been able to walk on the water thanks to the same accident of birth.

As we travelled, we heard about the Grande Armée, how many thousands had died and I was sick to hear of so much waste and for no purpose. Bonaparte said that a night in Paris with the whores would replenish every one. Maybe, but it would take seventeen years for them to grow up.

Even the French were beginning to get tired. Even the women without ambition wanted something more than to produce boys to be killed and girls to grow up to produce more boys. We were getting weary. Talleyrand wrote to the Czar and said, *The French people are civilised, their leader is not . . .*

We are not especially civilised, we wanted what he wanted for a long time. We wanted glory and conquest and slaves and praise. His desire burned for longer than ours because it was never likely that he would pay for it with his life. He kept his valuable, fabulous thing behind the secret panel until the last moment, but we, who had so little except our lives, were gambling with all we had from the start.

He saw what we felt.

He reflected on our losses.

He had tents and food when we were dying.

He was trying to found a dynasty. We were fighting for our lives.

There's no such thing as a limited victory. One conquest only leads on, ineluctably, to another, to protect what has been won. We found no friends of France on our journey, only crushed enemies. Enemies like you and me with the same hopes and fears, neither good nor bad. I had been taught to look for monsters and devils and I found ordinary people.

But the ordinary people were looking for devils too. The Austrians in particular believed the French to be brutal and beneath contempt. Still believing us to be Italian, they were generous to a fault and compared us favourably in every way with the French. And if I had thrown off my disguise? What then, would I have turned into a devil before their eyes? I worried that they would smell me, that their noses, so disdainful and attuned to hate anything that had a whiff of Bonaparte, would detect me straight away. But it seems we are as we appear. What a nonsense we make of our hatreds when we can only recognise them in the most obvious circumstances.

We were close to the Danube when Patrick began to behave oddly. We had been travelling for more than two months and we found ourselves in a valley surrounded by pine forests. We were at the bottom like ants in a great green cage. We were making good time now that we were out of the snow and the worst of the cold. Our spirits were high; another two weeks perhaps and we might reach Italy. Patrick had been singing songs since we left Moscow. Unintelligible, tuneless songs but sounds we had grown accustomed to, that we marched to. For the last day or so he had been silent, hardly eating and not wanting to talk. As we sat around our fire in the valley that night, he started to talk about Ireland and how much he wanted to be home. He was wondering whether or not he could persuade the Bishop to give him a parish again. He had liked being a priest, 'And not just for the girls, though there was that, I know.'

He said it made sense, whether you believed or not, it made sense to go to church and think about someone who wasn't your family or your enemy.

I said it was hypocritical and he said Domino was right about me; that I was a puritan at heart, didn't understand weakness and mess and simple humanness.

I was very much hurt by this, but I think what he said was true and it is a fault in me.

Villanelle told us about the churches in Venice with their paintings of angels and devils and thieving men and adulterous women and animals everywhere. Patrick brightened and thought he might try his luck in Venice first.

He woke me in the middle of the night. He was raving. I tried to hold him down, but he's strong and neither I nor Villanelle dared risk his flailing fists and feet. He was sweating despite the cold night and there was blood on his lips. We piled our blankets over him and I set off into the dark that still terrified me to find more dry wood and build up the fire. We built him a fiery furnace but he couldn't get warm. He sweated and shook and shouted that he was freezing to death, that the Devil had got into his lungs and was breathing damnation at him.

He died at about dawn.

We had no shovels, no way of penetrating the black earth, so we carried him between us to the beginning of the pine forests and covered him with bracken and branches and leaves. Buried him like a hedgehog waiting for summer.

Then we were afraid. What had he died of and could we have caught it? Despite the weather and our need to move on, we went to the river and washed ourselves and our clothes and shivered in the weak afternoon sun by the fire. Villanelle was talking gloomily about catarrh, but I knew nothing then of that Venetian disease that now attacks me every November.

When we left Patrick behind we left our optimism with him.

We had begun to believe that we would finish our journey

and now that seemed less possible. If one can go why not three? We tried to joke, remembering his face when the ox-boy had sat on him, remembering his wild sightings; he once claimed to have spotted the Blessed Virgin herself touring the heavens on a gilded donkey. He was always seeing things and it didn't matter how or what, it mattered that he saw and that he told us stories. Stories were all we had.

He had told us the story of his miraculous eye and when he had first discovered it. It was on a hot morning in County Cork and the church doors were wide open to let out the heat and the smell of sweat that even a good wash can't get rid of after six days in the fields. Patrick was preaching a fine sermon about Hell and the perils of the flesh and his eyes roamed the congregation; at least his right eye did, he found that his left eye was focused three fields away on a pair of his parishioners who were committing adultery under God's Heaven while their spouses knelt in his church.

After the sermon, Patrick was deeply perplexed. Had he seen them or was he like St Jerome and subject to lustful visions? He walked round to visit them that afternoon and, after a few chance remarks, judged from their guilty faces that they had indeed been doing what he thought they'd been doing.

There was a woman of the parish, very devout with a bosom that preceded her, and Patrick found by standing in his little manse he could see straight into her bedroom without any vulgar telescope. He did look occasionally, just to check that she wasn't in sin. He reckoned, after all, that the Lord must have granted him this eye for some righteous purpose.

Hadn't he granted Samson strength?

'And Samson was a one for the women too.'

Could he see us now? Could he look down from his place next to the Blessed Virgin and see us walking away thinking of him?

Perhaps both his eyes were now far-sighted. I wanted him to be in Heaven even though I didn't believe there could be such a place.

I wanted him to see us home.

Many of my friends were dead. There was only one boy left of those five of us who had laughed at the red barn and the cows we had birthed. Others I had come to know over the years and grown used to had been fatally wounded or recorded missing on one battlefield or another. A fighting man is careful not to make too many ties. I saw a cannonball blow a stonemason in two, a man I liked and I tried to drag his two halves off the field, but when I came back for his legs they were indistinguishable from the other legs. There was a carpenter they had shot for carving a rabbit out of his musket-butt.

Death in battle seemed glorious when we were not in battle. But for the men who were bloodied and maimed and made to run through smoke that choked them into enemy lines where bayonets were waiting, death in battle seemed only what it was. Death. The curious thing is that we always went back. The Grande Armée had more recruits than it could train and very few desertions, at least until recently. Bonaparte said war was in our blood.

Could that be true?

And if it is true there will be no end to these wars. Not now, not ever. Whenever we shout Peace! and run home to our sweethearts and till the land we will be not in peace but in a respite from the war to come. War will always be in the future. The future crossed out.

It can't be in our blood.

Why would a people who love the grape and the sun die in the zero winter for one man?

Why did I? Because I loved him. He was my passion and when we go to war we feel we are not a lukewarm people any more.

What did Villanelle think?

Men are violent. That's all there is to it.

Being with her was like pressing your eye to a particularly vivid kaleidoscope. She was all primary colour and although she understood better than I the ambiguities of the heart she was not equivocal in her thinking.

'I come from the city of mazes,' she said, 'but if you ask me a direction I will tell you straight ahead.'

We were now in the Kingdom of Italy, and it was her plan to take a boat to Venice, where we could stay with her family until it was safe for me to return to France. In return, she would ask of me a favour and that favour concerned the re-possession of her heart.

'My lover still has it. I left it there. I want you to help me get it back.'

I promised her my help but there was something I wanted too; why had she never taken her boots off? Not even while we stayed with the peasants in Russia? Not even in bed?

She laughed and drew back her hair, and her eyes were bright with two deep furrows between the eyebrows. I thought she was the most beautiful woman I had ever seen.

'I told you. My father was a boatman. Boatmen do not take off their boots,' and that was all she would say, but I determined on my arrival in her enchanted city to find out more about these boatmen and their boots.

We were fortunate in a fair passage and on that calm glittering sea the war and the winter seemed years away. Someone else's past. And so it was that in May 1813 I had my first glimpse of Venice.

Arriving at Venice by sea, as one must, is like seeing an invented city rise up and quiver in the air. It is a trick of the early light to make the buildings shimmer so that they seem never still. It is not built on any lines I can fathom but rather seems to have pushed itself out, impudently, here and there. To have swelled like yeast in a shape of its own. There are no preliminaries, no docks for the smaller craft, your boat anchors in the lagoon and in a moment with no more ado you are in St Mark's Square. I watched Villanelle's face; the face of someone coming home, seeing nothing but the homecoming. Her eyes flickered from the domes to cats, embracing what she saw and passing a silent message that she was back. I envied her that. I was still an exile.

We landed and taking my hand she led me through an impossible maze, past something I seemed to translate as the Bridge of Fists and even more unlikely, the Canal of the Toilet, until we arrived at a quiet waterway.

'This is the back of my house,' she said, 'the front door is on the canal.'

Their front doors opened into the water?

Her mother and stepfather greeted us with the kind of rapture I had always imagined to have been the luck of the Prodigal Son. They drew up chairs and sat close by so that all our knees touched and her mother kept leaping up and running out to fetch trays of cakes and jugs of wine. At every one of our stories, her father slapped me on the back and went 'Ha Ha', and her mother raised her hands to the Madonna and said, 'What a mercy you are here.'

The fact that I was a Frenchman didn't bother them at all. 'Not every Frenchman is Napoleon Bonaparte,' said her father. 'I have known some good ones, though Villanelle's husband was not such a good one.'

I looked at her startled. She had never said that her fat husband was a Frenchman. I presumed her facility for my language had come with living around so many soldiers for most of her life.

She shrugged, her usual gesture when she didn't want to explain and asked what had happened to her husband.

'He comes and goes, like always, but you can hide.'

The thought of hiding the two of us, fugitives for different reasons, appealed enormously to Villanelle's parents.

'When I was married to a boatman,' said her mother, 'things were happening every day, but the boat people are clannish and now that I am married to a baker,' she tweaked his cheek, 'they go their ways and I go mine.' Her eyes narrowed and she leaned forwards so close that I could smell her breakfast. 'There are stories I could tell you, Henri, that would make your hair stand on end,' and she slapped me on the knee so violently that I fell back in my chair.

'Leave the boy alone,' said her husband, 'he's just walked from Moscow.'

'Madonna,' exclaimed she, 'how could I?' and she forced me to eat another cake.

When I was reeling with cakes and wine and almost collapsed with exhaustion, she took me around the house and showed me in particular the little grille with a mirror positioned at such an angle as to reveal the identity of any caller at the water-gate.

'We won't always be here and you must be sure who it is if you are to open the door. As a further precaution I think you should shave off your beard. We Venetians are not hairy and you will stand out.'

I thanked her and slept for two days.

On the third day I awoke to a quiet house and my room completely dark because the shutters were so tightly closed. I threw them back and let in the yellow light that touched my face and broke in spears across the floor. I could see the dust in the sunlight. The room was low and uneven and the walls had faded spaces where pictures had hung. There was a wash-stand and a full jug, ice cold, and after so much cold and in this warmth, I could only bear to dip in my fingers and rub away the sleep from my eyes. There was a mirror too. Full length on a wooden swivel stand. The mirror was silvered in places, but I saw myself, thin and bony, with a too large head and a ruffian's beard. They were right. I must shave before I went out. From my window which overlooked the canal I saw a whole world going about in boats. Vegetable boats, passenger boats, boats with canopies covering rich ladies and bones as thin as a knife-blade with raised prows. These were the strangest boats of all because their owners rowed them standing up. As far as I could see, the canal was marked at regular intervals with gaily striped poles, some with boats butting against them, others, their gold tops peeling in the sun.

I threw the filthy water I used along with the remains of my beard into the canal and prayed that my past had sunk for ever.

I got lost from the first. Where Bonaparte goes, straight roads follow, buildings are rationalised, street signs may change to celebrate a battle but they are always clearly marked. Here, if they bother with street signs at all, they are happy to use the same ones over again. Not even Bonaparte could rationalise Venice.

This is a city of madmen.

Everywhere, I found a church and sometimes it seemed I found the same square but with different churches. Perhaps here churches spring up overnight like mushrooms and dissolve as quickly with the dawn. Perhaps the Venetians build them overnight? At the height of their powers they built a galleon every day, fully fitted. Why not a church, fully fitted? The only rational place in the whole city is the public garden and even there, on a foggy night, four sepulchral churches rise up and swamp the regimental pines.

I did not return to the baker's home for five days because I could not find my way and because I felt embarrassed to speak French to these people. I walked, looking for bread stalls, sniffing like a tracker dog, hoping to catch a clue on the air. But I only found churches.

At last, I turned a corner, a corner I swear I had turned a hundred times before and I saw Villanelle plaiting her hair in a boat.

'We thought you'd gone back to France,' she said. 'Mama was broken hearted. She wants you to be her son.'

'I need a map.'

'It won't help. This is a living city. Things change.'

'Villanelle, cities don't.'

'Henri, they do.'

She ordered me into the boat, promising food on the way.

'I'll take you on a tour, then you won't go missing again.'

The boat smelled of urine and cabbages and I asked her whose it was. She said it belonged to a man who bred bears. An admirer of hers. I was learning not to ask her too many questions; truth or lie, the answers were usually unsatisfactory.

We slid out of the sun, down icy tunnels that set my teeth on edge and past damp worker barges, hauled up with their nameless cargo.

'This city enfolds upon itself. Canals hide other canals, alleyways cross and criss-cross so that you will not know which is which until you have lived here all your life. Even when you have mastered the squares and you can pass from the Rialto to the Ghetto and out to the lagoon with confidence, there will still be places you can never find and if you do find them you may never see St Mark's again. Leave plenty of time in your doings and be prepared to go another way, to do something not planned if that is where the streets lead you.'

We rowed in a shape that seemed to be a figure of eight working back on itself. When I suggested to Villanelle that she was being deliberately mysterious and taking me a way I would never recognise again, she smiled and said she was taking me down an ancient way that only a boatman could hope to remember.

'The cities of the interior do not lie on any map.'

We passed ransacked palaces, their curtains swinging from shutterless windows and now and again I caught sight of a lean figure on a broken balcony.

'These are the exiles, the people the French drove out. These people are dead but they do not disappear.'

We passed a group of children whose faces were old and evil.

'I'm taking you to see my friend.'

The canal she turned into was littered with waste and rats floating pink belly up. At times it was almost too narrow for us to pass and she pushed off the walls, her oar scraping generations of slime. No one could live here.

'What time might it be?'

Villanelle laughed. 'Visiting time. I've brought a friend.'

She drew in her boat to a stinking recess and squatting on a ledge of precariously floating crates was a woman so sunken and filthy that I scarcely thought her a human at all. Her hair was glowing, some curious phosphorescent mould clung to it and gave her the appearance of a subterranean devil. She was dressed in folds of a heavy material, impossible to place in colour or design. One of her hands had only three fingers.

'I've been away,' said Villanelle. 'Away a long time, but I won't go away again. This is Henri.'

The old creature continued to regard Villanelle. She spoke. 'You've been away as you tell me and I have watched for you while you were gone and sometimes seen your ghost floating this way. You have been in danger and there is more to come but you will not leave again. Not in this life.'

There was no light where we sat huddled. The buildings on either side of the water closed in like an arch above our heads. So close that the roofs seemed to touch in places. Were we in the sewers? 'I brought you fish.' Villanelle took out a parcel which the old woman sniffed before putting beneath her skirts. Then she turned to me.

'Beware of old enemies in new disguises.'

'Who is she?' I asked as soon as we were safely away.

Villanelle shrugged and I knew I would get no real answer. 'She's an exile. She used to live there,' and she pointed out a forgotten building with a double water-gate that had been left to sink so that the waters now lapped into the lower rooms. The top floors were used for storage and a pulley hung out of one of the windows.

'When she lived there, they say the lights never went out before dawn and the cellars had wines so rare that a man might die if he drank more than a glass. She kept ships on the seas and the ships brought home commodities that made her one of the wealthiest women in Venice. When others talked of her, they did so with respect and when they referred to her husband they called him "The Husband of the Lady of Means". She lost her means when Bonaparte took a fancy to them and they say that Joséphine has her jewels.'

'Joséphine has most people's jewels,' I said.

We rowed out of the hidden city into squares of sunlight and wide canals that hugged the boats eight or nine across and still left room for the flimsy pleasure craft of the visitors. 'This is the time of year for them. And if you stay till August you can celebrate Bonaparte's birthday. But he may be dead by then. In that case you must certainly stay till August and we'll celebrate his funeral.'

She had stopped our boat outside an imposing residence that rose up six floors and commanded a choice place on this clean and fashionable canal.

'In that house, you will find my heart. You must break in, Henri, and get it back for me.'

Was she mad? We had been talking figuratively. Her heart was in her body like mine. I tried to explain this to her, but she took my hand and put it against her chest.

'Feel for yourself.'

I felt and without the slightest subterfuge moved my hand up and down. I could feel nothing. I put my ear to her body and crouched quite still in the bottom of the boat and a passing gondolier gave us a knowing smile.

I could hear nothing.

'Villanelle, you'd be dead if you had no heart.'

'Those soldiers you lived with, do you think they had hearts? Do you think my fat husband has a heart somewhere in his lard?' Now it was me shrugging my shoulders. 'It's a way of putting it, you know that.'

'I know that but I've told you already. This is an unusual city, we do things differently here.'

'You want me to go inside that house and search for your heart?'

'Yes.'

It was fantastic.

'Henri, when you left Moscow, Domino gave you an icicle with a thread of gold running through it. Where is it?'

I told her I didn't know what had happened to it, I guessed it had melted in my pack and I had lost the thread of gold. I was ashamed of having lost it, but when Patrick died I forgot to take care of the things I loved for a while.

'I have it.'

'You have the gold?' I was incredulous, relieved. She must have found it and so I hadn't lost Domino after all.

'I have the icicle.' She fished into her bag and drew it out as cold and hard as the day he had plucked it from the canvas and sent me away. I turned it over in my hands. The boat bobbed up and down and the seagulls went their ordinary way. I looked at her, my eyes full of questions, but she only drew up her shoulders and turned her face back towards the house. 'Tonight, Henri. Tonight they'll be at the Fenice. I'll bring you here and wait for you, but I'm afraid to go in in case I can't bring myself to leave again.'

She took the icicle from me. 'When you bring me my heart, I'll give you your miracle.'

'I love you,' I said.

'You're my brother,' she said and we rowed away.

We ate supper together, she, me and her parents, and they pressed me for details of my family.

'I come from a village surrounded by hills that stretch away bright green and spattered with dandelions. There is a river runs by that floods its banks every winter and chokes in mud every summer. We depend on the river. We depend on the sun. There are no streets and squares where I come from, only small houses, one storey usually and paths in between made by so many feet not so many designing hands. We have no church, we use the barn, and in winter we have to squeeze in with the hay. We didn't notice the Revolution. Like you, it took us by surprise. Our thoughts are on the wood in our hands and the grain we grow and now and again on God. My mother was a devout woman and when she died my father said she was holding out her arms to the Holy Mother and her face was lit up from within. She died by chance. A horse fell on her and broke her hip and we have no medicine for such things, only for colic and madness. That was two years ago. My father still draws the plough and catches the moles that gash the fields. If I can, I'll get home for harvest and help him. It's where I belong.'

'What about your brains, Henri?' asked Villanelle, half sarcastic. 'A man like you, taught by a priest and travelled and fought. What will you think about back with the cattle?'

I shrugged. 'What use are brains?'

'You could make your fortune here,' said her father, 'there's chances here for a young man.'

'You can stay with us,' said her mother.

But she said nothing and I could not stay and be her brother when my heart cried out to love her.

'You know,' said her mother, catching my arm, 'this is not a city like any other. Paris? I spit on it.' She spat. 'What's Paris? Just a few boulevards and some expensive shops. Here, there are mysteries that only the dead know. I tell you, the boatmen here have webbed feet. No, don't smile, it's true. I was married to one that's how I know and I brought up sons by my previous marriage.' She poked her foot in the air and tried to reach her toes. 'In between each toe, you'll find a web and with those webs they walk on water.'

Her husband didn't roar and bang the water jug as he usually did when he found something funny. He met my eyes and gave his little half smile.

'A man has to keep an open mind. Ask Villanelle.'

But she was tight-lipped and soon left the room.

'She needs a new husband,' said her mother, her voice almost pleading, 'once that man's out of the way . . . accidents happen very often in Venice, it's so dark and the waters are so deep. Who would be surprised if there was another death?'

Her husband laid his hand on her arm. 'Don't tempt the spirits.'

After the meal was over and her father was snoozing while her mother embroidered a cloth, Villanelle led me down to the boat and we slipped black along the black water. She had exchanged her cabbage and urine boat for a gondola and she rowed standing up in their off-centre graceful way. She said it was a better disguise; gondoliers often hung round the grand houses hoping for business. I was about to ask her where she had got the boat, but the words died in my mouth when I saw the markings on the prow.

It was a funeral boat.

The night was chilly but not dark with a bright moon that cast our shadows grotesquely on the water. We were soon at the water-gate and, as she had promised, the house seemed empty.

'How will I get in?' I whispered as she tied her boat to an iron ring.

'With this.' She gave me a key. Smooth and flat like a gaoler's key. 'I kept it for luck. It never brought me any.'

'How will I find your heart? This house is six storeys.'

'Listen for it beating and look in unlikely places. If there's danger, you'll hear me cry like a seagull over the water and you must hurry back.'

I left her and stepped into the wide hall, coming face to face with a full-sized scaly beast with a horn protruding from its head. I gave a little cry, but it was stuffed. In front of me was a wooden staircase that bent round half-way up and disappeared into the middle of the house. I determined to start at the top and make my way down. I expected to find nothing, but unless I was able to describe each room to Villanelle, she would force me here again. I was certain of that.

The first door I opened had nothing in it but a harpsichord.

The second had fifteen stained-glass windows.

The third had no windows and on the floor, side by side, were two coffins, their lids open, white silk inside.

The fourth room was shelved from floor to ceiling and those shelves were filled with books two deep. There was a ladder.

In the fifth room a light burned and covering the whole of one wall was a map of the world. A map with whales in the seas and terrible monsters chewing the land. There were roads marked that seemed to disappear into the earth and at other times to stop abruptly at the sea's edge. In each corner sat a cormorant, a fish struggling in its beak.

The sixth room was a sewing room, a tapestry some three-quarters done lay in its frame. The picture was of a young woman cross-legged in front of a pack of cards. It was Villanelle.

The seventh room was a study; the desk was covered in

journals covered in a tiny spidery hand. Writing I could not read.

The eighth room had only a billiard table and a little door leading off at one side. I was drawn to this door and, opening it, found it to be a vast walk-in closet racked with dresses of every kind, smelling of musk and incense. A woman's room. Here, I felt no fear. I wanted to bury my face in the clothes and lie on the floor with the smell about me. I thought of Villanelle and her hair across my face and wondered if that was how she had felt with this sweet-smelling, seductive woman. Around the sides of the room were ebony boxes, monogrammed. I opened one and found it packed with little glass phials. Inside were the aromas of pleasure and danger. Each phial contained at most five drops and so I judged them to be essences of great value and potency. Hardly thinking, I put one in my pocket and turned to leave. As I did so, a noise stopped me. A noise not like the sound of mice or beetles. A regular steady noise, like a heartbeat. My own heart missed a beat and I began to fling back gown after gown, scattering shoes and underclothes in my haste. I sat on my heels and listened again. It was low down, concealed.

On my hands and knees I crawled under one of the clothes rails and found a silk shift wrapped round an indigo jar. The jar was throbbing. I did not dare to unstopper it. I did not dare to check this valuable, fabulous thing and I carried it, still in the shift, down the last two floors and out into the empty night.

Villanelle was hunched in the boat staring at the water. When she heard me she reached out her hand to steady me and without asking a question rowed us swiftly away and far out into the lagoon. When she stopped at last, her sweat shining pale under the moon, I handed her my bundle.

She gave a sigh and her hands trembled, then she bade me turn away.

I heard her uncork the jar and a sound like gas escaping. Then she began to make terrible swallowing and choking noises and only my fear kept me sitting at the other end of the boat, perhaps hearing her die.

There was quiet. She touched my back and when I turned round took my hand again and placed it on her breast.

Her heart was beating.

Not possible.

I tell you her heart was beating.

She asked me for the key and, placing both the key and the shift in the indigo jar, she tossed it into the water and smiled such a smile of radiance that had this all been folly, it would have been worth it. She asked me what I saw and I told her of each room and at each room she asked of another room and then I told her about the tapestry. Her face whitened.

'But you say it was not finished?'

'It was three-quarters finished.'

'And it was me? You're sure?'

Why was she so upset? Because if the tapestry had been finished and the woman had woven in her heart, she would have been a prisoner for ever.

'I don't understand any of this, Villanelle.'

'Don't think about it any more, I have my heart, you have your miracle. Now we can enjoy ourselves,' and she unravelled her hair and rowed me home in her red forest.

I slept badly, dreaming of the old woman's words, 'Beware of old enemies in new disguises,' but in the morning when Villa-nelle's mother woke me with eggs and coffee, the night gone and its nightmares seemed part of the same fantasy.

This is the city of madmen.

Her mother sat by my bed and chatted and urged me to ask Villanelle to marry me when she was free.

'I had a dream last night,' she said. 'A dream of death. Ask her, Henri.'

When we were out together that afternoon I did ask her, but she shook her head.

'I can't give you my heart.'

'I don't have to have it.'

'Perhaps not, but I need to give it. You're my brother.'

When I told her mother what had happened, she stopped in her baking. 'You're too steady for her, she goes for madmen. I tell her to calm down but she never will. She wants it to be Pentecost every day.'

Then she muttered something about the terrible island and blamed herself, but I never question these Venetians when they mutter; it's their own affair.

I began to think of leaving for France and though the thought of not seeing her each day froze my heart more cleanly than any zero winter, I remembered words of hers, words she had used when Patrick and she and I lay in a Russian hut drinking evil spirit . . .

There's no sense in loving someone you can only wake up to by chance.

They say this city can absorb anyone. It does seem that every nationality is here in some part. There are dreamers and poets and landscape painters with dirty noses and wanderers like me who came here by chance and never left. They are all looking for something, travelling the world and the seven seas but looking for a reason to stay. I'm not looking, I've found what it is I want and I can't have it. If I stayed, I would be staying not out of hope but out of fear. Fear of being alone, of being parted from a woman who simply by her presence makes the rest of my life seem shadows.

I say I'm in love with her. What does that mean?

It means I review my future and my past in the light of this feeling. It is as though I wrote in a foreign language that I am suddenly able to read. Wordlessly, she explains me to myself. Like genius, she is ignorant of what she does.

I was a bad soldier because I cared too much about what

happened next. I could never lose myself in the cannonfire, in the moment of combat and hate. My mind ran before me with pictures of dead fields and all that had taken years to make, lost in a day or so.

I stayed because I had nowhere else to go.

I don't want to do that again.

Do all lovers feel helpless and valiant in the presence of the beloved? Helpless because the need to roll over like a pet dog is never far away. Valiant because you know you would slay a dragon with a pocket knife if you had to.

When I dream of a future in her arms no dark days appear, not even a head cold, and though I know it's nonsense I really believe we would always be happy and that our children would change the world.

I sound like those soldiers who dream of home . . .

No. She'd vanish for days at a time and I'd weep. She'd forget we had any children and leave me to take care of them. She'd gamble our house away at the Casino, and if I took her to live in France she'd grow to hate me.

I know all this and it makes no difference.

She'd never be faithful.

She'd laugh in my face.

I will always be afraid of her body because of the power it has.

And in spite of these things when I think of leaving, my chest is full of stones.

Infatuation. First love. Lust.

My passion can be explained away. But this is sure: whatever she touches, she reveals.

I think about her body a lot; not possessing it but watching it twist in sleep. She is never still; whether it be in boats or running full tilt with an armful of cabbages. She's not nervous, it's unnatural for her to be still. When I told her how much I like to lie in a bright green field watching the bright blue sky she said, 'You can do that when you're dead, tell them to leave the top off your coffin.'

But she knows about the sky. I can see her from my window in her boat rowing very slowly looking up at the faultless blue for the first star.

She decided to teach me to row. Not just row. Venetian row. We set off at dawn in a red gondola that the police used. I didn't bother to ask how she'd got it. She was so happy these days and often she took my hand and put it to her heart as though she were a patient given a second chance.

'If you're determined to be a goatherd after all, the least I can do is send you home with one real skill. You can make a boat in your quiet moments and sail down that river you talk about and think of me.'

'You could come with me if you liked.'

'I wouldn't like. What would I do with a sackful of moles and not a gaming table in sight?'

I knew it but I hated hearing it.

I was not a natural rower and more than once I tipped the boat so badly that both of us fell in and Villanelle grabbed me by the scruff of the neck and screamed she was drowning. 'You live on the water,' I protested when she dragged me under, yelling at the top of her voice.

'That's right. I live on it, I don't live in it.'

Amazingly, she couldn't swim.

'Boatmen don't need to swim. No boatman would end up like this. We can't go home till we're dry, I'll be made fun of.'

Not even her enthusiasm could help me get it right and at evening she snatched back the oars, her hair still damp, and told me we were going to the Casino instead.

'Maybe that's what you're good at.'

I had never been to a Casino before and I was disappointed the way the brothel had disappointed me years earlier. Sinful places are always so much more sinful in the imagination. There's no red plush as shockingly red as the red you dream up. No women with legs as long as you think they'll be. And in the mind these places are always free.

'There's a whipping room upstairs,' she said, 'if you're interested.' No. I'd be bored. I knew about whipping. I'd heard it all from my friend the priest. Saints love to be whipped and I've seen pictures galore of their extatic scars and longing glances. Watching an ordinary person being whipped couldn't have the same effect. Saintly flesh is soft and white and always hidden from the day. When the whip finds it out, that is the moment of pleasure, the moment when what was hidden is revealed.

I left her to it and when I'd seen what there was to see of cold marble and iced glasses and scarred baize, I retreated to a window seat and rested my mind on the shining canal below.

So the past had gone. I had escaped. Such things are possible.

I thought of my village and the bonfire we hold at the end of winter; doing away with the things we no longer need; celebrating the life to come. Eight soldier years had gone into the canal with the beard that didn't suit me. Eight years of Bonaparte. I saw my reflection in the window; this was the face I had become. Beyond my reflection I saw Villanelle backed up against the wall with a man standing in front of her blocking her way. She was watching him evenly, but I could see by the lift of her shoulders that she was afraid.

He was very wide, a great black expanse like a matador's cloak.

He stood with his feet planted apart, one arm leaning on the wall blocking her way, the other fixed in his pocket. She pushed him, swiftly and suddenly, and just as swiftly his hand flew from his pocket and slapped her. I heard the noise and, as I jumped up, she ducked under his arm and ran past me down the stairs. I could think of nothing but getting to her before he did and he was already in pursuit. I opened the window and jumped into the canal.

I came spluttering to the surface with a faceful of weed and swam to our boat, loosening the tie, so that when she leapt in like a cat, I was shouting at her to row and trying to scramble over the side. She ignored me and rowed and I was dragged behind like the tame dolphin a man on the Rialto keeps.

'It's him,' she said, as I finally tumbled in a heap at her feet. 'I thought he was still away, my spies are good.'

'Your husband?'

She spat. 'My greasy, cock-sucking husband, yes.'

I sat up. 'He's following us.'

'I know a way; I'm a boatman's daughter.'

I grew dizzy with the circles she rowed and the speed she rowed at. The muscles in her arms stood out threatening to break the skin and when we passed some light I saw the outcrop of her veins. She was breathing hard, her body was soon as wet as mine. We were heading down a stretch of water that got narrower and narrower and stopped absolutely in a blank white wall. At the last second, when I expected to hear our boat splinter like driftwood, Villanelle swung an impossible curve and pulled us up an inlet that led through a dripping tunnel.

'Home soon, Henri, keep calm.'

It was the first time I had ever heard her use the word calm.

We pulled up against her water-gate but, as we prepared to fasten our boat, a silent prow slid from behind us and I was staring into the face of the cook.

The cook.

The flesh around his mouth moved into a suggestion of a smile. He was much heavier than when I had known him, with jowls that hung like dead moles and a plump case of skin that held his head to his shoulders. His eyes had receded and his eyebrows, always thick, now loomed at me like sentries. He folded his hands on the edge of the boat, hands with rings forced over the knuckles. Red hands.

'Henri,' he said. 'My pleasure.'

Villanelle's questioning look to me wrestled with her look of pure disgust fixed on him. He saw her conflict and touching her lightly so that she winced said, 'You could say Henri was my good luck. Thanks to him and his little tricks I was drummed out of Boulogne and sent to Paris to mind the Stores. I've never been one to mind anything that didn't have something in it for me. Aren't you pleased, Henri, to meet an old friend and see him so prosperous?'

'I don't want anything to do with you,' I said.

He smiled again and I saw his teeth this time. What was left of them. 'But you do, you clearly want something to do with my wife. My wife,' and he enunciated the words very slowly. Then his face took on an old expression, I knew it well. 'I'm surprised to see you here, Henri. Shouldn't you be with your regiment? This is not a time for holidaying, not even if you're a favourite of Bonaparte's.'

'It's none of your business.'

'Indeed not, but you won't mind me mentioning you to a few of my friends, will you?'

He turned to Villanelle. 'I have other friends who'll be interested to know what's happened to you. Friends who paid a lot of money to get to know you. It will be easier if you come with me now.'

She spat in his face.

What happened next is still not clear to me even though I have had years to think about it. Calm years with no distraction. I remember he leaned forward when she spat and tried to kiss her. I remember his mouth opening and coming towards her, his hands loosed from the boat side, his body bent. His hand scraped her breast. His mouth. His mouth is the clearest image I have. A pale pink mouth, a cavern of flesh and then his tongue, just visible like a worm from its hole. She pushed him and he lost balance between the two boats and fell on to me, nearly crushing me. He put his hands to my throat and I heard Villanelle cry out and throw her knife towards me, within reach. A Venetian knife, thin and cruel.

'Soft side, Henri, like sea urchins.'

I had the knife in my hand and I thrust it at his side. As he rolled I thrust it in his belly. I heard it suckle his guts. I pulled it out, angry knife at being so torn away, and I let it go in again, through the years of good living. That goose and claret flesh soon fell away. My shirt was soaked in blood. Villanelle dragged him off me, half off me, and I stood up, not unsteady at all. I told her to help me turn him over and she did so, watching me.

When we had him belly up and running blood I tore his shirt from the collar down and looked at his chest. Hairless and white, like the flesh of saints. Can saints and devils be so alike? His nipples were the same shade as his lips.

'You said he had no heart, Villanelle, let's see.'

She put her hand out, but I had already made a rip with my silver friend, such an eager blade. I cut a triangle in about the right place and scooped out the shape with my hand, like coring an apple.

He had a heart.

'Do you want it, Villanelle?'

She shook her head and started to cry. I had never seen her cry, not through the zero winter, not at the death of our friend, not in the teeth of humiliation nor the telling of it. She was crying now and I took her in my arms dropping the heart between us and told her a story about a Princess whose tears turned to jewels.

'I've dirtied your clothes,' I said, seeing for the first time the smears of blood on her. 'Look at my hands.'

She nodded and the blue and bloody thing lay between us.

'We have to get these boats away, Henri.'

But in the struggle we had lost both of our oars and one of his. She took my head in her hands and weighed it, held me tight under the chin. 'Sit still, you've done what you could, now let me do what I can.'

I sat with my head on my knees, my eyes fixed on the floor of the boat that swam with blood. My feet rested in blood.

The cook, face up, had his eyes fixed on God.

Our boats were moving. I saw his boat in front of me gliding ahead, mine tied to it the way children tie their boats on a pond.

We were moving. How?

I raised my head fully, my knees still drawn up, and saw Villanelle, her back towards me, a rope over her shoulder, walking on the canal and dragging our boats.

Her boots lay neatly one by the other. Her hair was down.

I was in the red forest and she was leading me home.

· 4 ·

the Rock

They say the dead don't talk. Silent as the grave they say. It's not true. The dead are talking all the time. On this rock, when the wind is up, I can hear them.

I can hear Bonaparte; he didn't last long on his rock. He put on weight and caught a cold, and he who survived the plagues of Egypt and the zero winter died in the mild damp.

The Russians invaded Paris and we didn't burn it down, we gave it up and they took him away and restored the monarchy.

His heart sang. On a windy island in the face of gulls, his heart sang. He waited for the moment and like the third son who knows his treacherous brothers won't outwit him, the moment came and in a salty convoy of silent boats he returned for a hundred days and met his Waterloo.

What could they do with him? These victorious Generals and self-righteous nations?

You play, you win, you play, you lose. You play.

The end of every game is an anti-climax. What you thought you would feel you don't feel, what you thought was so important isn't any more. It's the game that's exciting.

And if you win?

There's no such thing as a limited victory. You must protect what you have won. You must take it seriously.

Victors lose when they are tired of winning. Perhaps they regret it later, but the impulse to gamble the valuable, fabulous thing is too strong. The impulse to be reckless again, to go barefoot, like you used to, before you inherited all those shoes.

He never slept, he had an ulcer, he had divorced Joséphine and married a selfish bitch (though he deserved her), he needed a dynasty to protect his Empire. He had no friends. It took him about three minutes to have sex and increasingly he didn't even bother to unbuckle his sword. Europe hated him. The French were tired of going to war and going to war and going to war.

He was the most powerful man in the world.

Returning from that island the first time he felt like a boy again. A hero again with nothing to lose. A saviour with one change of clothes.

When they won hands down a second time and chose for him a darker rock where the tides were harsh and the company unsympathetic, they were burying him alive.

The Third Coalition. The forces of moderation against this madman.

I hated him, but they were no better. The dead are dead, whatever side they fight on.

Three madmen versus one madman. Numbers win. Not righteousness.

When the wind is up, I hear him weeping and he comes to me, his hands still greasy from his last dinner, and he asks me if I love him. His face pleads with me to say I do and I think of those who went into exile with him and one by one took a small boat home.

They had notebooks with them mostly. His life-story, his feelings on the rock. They were going to make their fortunes exhibiting this lamed beast.

Even his servants learned to write.

He talks about his past obsessively because the dead have no future and their present is recollection. They are in eternity because time has stopped.

Joséphine is still alive and has recently introduced the geranium to France. I mentioned this to him, but he said he never liked flowers.

My room here is very small. If I lie down, which I try not to do for reasons I will explain, I can touch each corner just by stretching out. I have a window though and, unlike most of the other windows here, it has no bars. It is perfectly open. It has no glass. I can lean right out and look across the lagoon and sometimes I see Villanelle in her boat.

She waves to me with her handkerchief.

In winter, I have a thick curtain made of sacks that I drape twice over the window and fasten to the floor with my commode. It works well enough providing I keep my blanket round me, though I suffer from catarrh. That proves I'm a Venetian now. There's straw on the floor, like at home, and some days when I wake, I can smell porridge cooking, thick and black. I like those days because it means mother is here. She looks just as always, perhaps a little younger. She walks with a limp where the horse fell on her, but she doesn't have to walk far in this little room.

We get bread for breakfast.

There isn't a bed, but there are two big pillows that were stuffed with straw too. Over the years I've filled them with seagull feathers and I sleep sitting on one, the other propped behind my back against the wall. It's comfortable and it means he can't strangle me.

When I first came here, I forget how many years I've been here, he tried to strangle me every night. I lay down in my shared room and I'd feel his hands on my throat and his breath that smelt of vomit and see his fleshy pink mouth, obscene rose pink, coming to kiss me.

They moved me to my own room after a while. I upset the others.

There's another man with his own room too. He's been here almost for ever and he's escaped a few times. They bring him back half drowned, he thinks he can walk on water. He has money and so his room is very comfortable. I could have money but I won't take it from her.

We hid the boats in a stinking passage where the garbage tugs go and Villanelle put her boots back on. It's the only time I've ever seen her feet and they are not what I'd usually call feet.

She unfolds them like a fan and folds them in on themselves in the same way. I wanted to touch but my hands were covered in blood. We left him where he lay, face up, his heart beside him, and Villanelle wrapped me to her as we walked, to comfort me and to conceal some of the blood on my clothes. When we passed anyone she threw me against the wall and kissed me passionately, blocking all sight of my body. In this way we made love.

She told her parents all that had taken place and the three of them drew hot water and washed me and burned my clothes.

'I dreamed of a death,' said her mother.

'Hush,' said her father.

They wrapped me in a fleece and put me to sleep by the stove on a mattress of her brother's, and I slept the sleep of the innocent and did not know that Villanelle kept silent vigil beside me all night. In my dreams I heard them say, 'What shall we do?'

'The authorities will come here. I am his wife. Take no part in it.'

'What about Henri? He's a Frenchman even if he isn't guilty.'

'I will take care of Henri.'

And when I heard those words I slept fully.

I think we knew we'd be caught.

We spent the few days that followed cramming our bodies with pleasure. We set out early each morning and rioted in the churches. That is to say, Villanelle basked in the colour and drama of God without giving God a thought and I sat on the steps playing noughts and crosses.

We ran our hands over every warm surface and soaked up the sun from iron and wood and the baking fur of millions of cats.

We ate fish fresh caught. She rowed me round the island in a pageant boat borrowed from a Bishop.

On the second night incessant summer rain flooded St Mark's Square and we stood on the edge watching a pair of Venetians weave their way across by means of two chairs.

'On my back,' I said.

She looked at me in disbelief.

'I can't walk on water but I can wade through it,' and I took off my shoes and made her carry them while we stumbled slowly across the wide Square. Her legs were so long that she had to keep hitching them up to stop them trailing in the water. When we reached the other side I was exhausted.

'This is the boy that walked from Moscow,' she taunted.

We linked arms and went in search of supper and after supper she showed me how to eat artichoke.

Pleasure and danger. Pleasure on the edge of danger is sweet. It's the gambler's sense of losing that makes the winning an act of love. On the fifth day, when our hearts had almost stopped knocking, we were almost casual about the sunset. The dull headache I'd had since I killed him had gone.

And on the sixth day they came for us.

They came early, as early as the vegetable boats on their way to market. They came without warning. Three of them, in a shiny black boat with a flag. Questioning they said, nothing more. Did Villanelle know her husband was dead? What happened after she and I left the Casino so hurriedly?

Had he followed? Had we seen him?

It seemed that Villanelle as his lawful undisputed wife was now to be in possession of a considerable fortune, unless of course, she was a murderess. There were papers for her to sign concerning his estate and she was led away to identify the body. I was advised not to leave the house, and to make sure that I took this advice a man stayed at the water-gate, enjoying the sun on his forehead.

I wished I were in a bright green field staring at the bright blue sky.

She did not return that night nor the night after and the man by the water-gate waited. When she did come home on the third morning, she was with the two men and her eyes were warning me, but she couldn't speak and so I was led away in silence. The cook's lawyer, a wily bent man with a wart on his cheek and beautiful hands, told me quite simply that he believed Villanelle to be guilty and believed me to be an accessory. Would I sign a statement saying so? If I would then he could probably look the other way while I disappeared.

'We are not unsubtle, we Venetians,' he said.

And what would happen to Villanelle?

The terms of the cook's will were curious; he had made no attempt to rid his wife of her rights, nor to apportion his fortune to another. He had simply said that if she could not inherit for any reason (absence being one), he willed his estate in its entirety to the Church.

Since he must never have expected to see her again, why had he chosen the Church? Had he ever been inside one? My surprise must have been evident because the lawyer in his candid mood said the cook loved to watch the choirboys in their red clothes. If his face showed the hint of a smile, the hint of anything other than an acceptance of a religious disposition, he hid it immediately.

What was in it for him? I wondered. What did he care who got the money? He didn't look like a man with a conscience. And for the first time in my life I realised that I was the powerful one. I was the one who held the wild card.

'I killed him,' I said. 'I stabbed him and I cut out his heart. Shall I show you the shape I made in his chest?'

I drew in the dust on the window. A triangle with rough edges. 'His heart was blue. Did you know hearts are blue? Not red at all. A blue stone in a red forest.'

'You're insane,' said the lawyer. 'No sane man would kill like that.'

'No sane man would live like he did.'

Neither of us spoke. I heard his breathing, sharp, like sandpaper. He laid both hands over the confession ready for me to sign. Beautiful manicured hands, whiter than the paper they rested on. Where had he got them from? They couldn't be his by right.

'If you are telling me the truth . . . '

'Trust me.'

'Then you must stay here until I am ready for you.'

He got up and locked the door behind him, leaving me in his comfortable room of tobacco and leather with a bust of Caesar on the table and a ragged heart on the window-pane.

In the evening, Villanelle came. She came alone because she was already wielding the power of her inheritance. She had a jar of wine, a loaf of bread from the bakery and a basket of uncooked sardines. We sat together on the floor, like children whose uncle has left them in his study by mistake.

'Do you know what you're doing?' she said.

'I told the truth, that's all.'

'Henri, I don't have any idea what comes next. Piero (the lawyer) thinks you're insane and will suggest you are tried as such. I can't buy him off. He was a friend of my husband's. He still believes I'm responsible and all the red hair in the world and all the money I have won't stop him hurting you. He hates for hate's sake. There are people like that. People who have everything. Money, power, sex. When they have everything they play for more sophisticated stakes than the rest of us. There are no thrills left to that man. The sun will never rise and delight him. He will never be lost in a strange town and forced to ask his way. I can't buy him. I can't tempt him. He wants a life for a life. You or me. Let it be me.'

'You didn't kill him, I killed him. I'm not sorry.'

'I would have and it doesn't matter whose knife or whose hand. You killed him for my sake.'

'No, I killed him for myself. He made every good thing dirty.'

She took my hands. We both smelt of fish.

'Henri, if you are convicted as insane, they'll either hang you or send you to San Servelo. The madhouse on the island.'

'The one you showed me? The one that stares over the lagoon and catches the light?'

She nodded and I wondered what it would be like to live in one place again.

'What will you do, Villanelle?'

'With the money? Buy a house. I've done enough travelling. Find ways of getting you free. That is, if you choose to live.'

'Will I be able to choose?'

'That much I can afford. It's not up to Piero, it's up to the judge.'

It was dark. She lit the candles and propped me against her body. I laid my head on her heart and heard it beating, so steady, as if it had always been there. I had never lain like this with anyone but my mother. My mother who took me on her breast and whispered the scripture in my ear. She hoped I'd learn it that way, but I heard nothing except the fire spitting and the steam rising from the water she heated for my father's wash. I heard nothing but her heart and felt nothing but her softness.

'I love you,' I said, then and now.

We watched the candles make bigger and bigger shadows on the ceiling as the sky became completely dark. Piero had a palm in his room (got from some cringing exile no doubt), and the palm cast a jungle on the ceiling, a tangle of broad leaves that could easily hide a tiger. Caesar on the table had a profile to recommend him, and of my triangle nothing could be seen. The room smelled of fish and candlewax. We lay flat on the floor for a while and I said, 'See? Now you understand why I love to be still and look at the sky.'

'I'm only still when I'm unhappy. I don't dare move because moving will hasten another day. I imagine that if I'm absolutely still what I dread won't happen. The last night I spent with her, the ninth night, I tried not to move at all while she slept. I heard a story about the cold wastelands in the far north where the nights are six months long and I hoped for an ordinary miracle to take us there. Would time pass if I refused to let it?'

We didn't make love that night. Our bodies were too heavy.

I stood trial the next day and it was as Villanelle had predicted. I was declared insane and sentenced to life imprisonment in San Servelo. I was to go that afternoon. Piero looked disappointed, but neither Villanelle nor I looked at him.

'I'll be able to visit you in about a week and I'll be working for you, I'll get you out of there. Everyone can be bribed. Courage, Henri. We walked from Moscow. We can walk across the water.'

'You can.'

'We can.' She hugged me and promised to be at the lagoon before the grim boat sailed away. I had few possessions but I wanted Domino's talisman and a picture of the Madonna her mother had embroidered for me.

San Servelo. It used to be just for the rich and mad but Bonaparte, who was egalitarian about lunacy at least, opened it to the public and set aside funds for its upkeep. It was still faded splendour inside. The rich and mad like their comforts. There was a spacious visitors' room where a lady might take tea while her son sat opposite in a strait jacket. At one time the warders had worn uniform and shiny boots and any inmate who drooled on those boots was shut away for a week. Not many inmates drooled. There was a garden that no one tended any more. A matted acre of rockery and fading flowers. There were now two

wings. One for the remaining rich and mad and one for the
increasing numbers of poor and mad. Villanelle had sent instructions to have me put in the former, but I found out what it cost
and refused.

I prefer to be with the ordinary people anyway.

In England, they have a mad King that nobody locks up.

George III who addresses his Upper Chamber as 'My Lords
and peacocks'.

Who can fathom the English and their horseradish?

I did not feel afraid to be in such strange company.

I only began to feel afraid when the voices started, and after
the voices the dead themselves, walking the halls and watching
me with their hollow eyes.

When Villanelle came the first few times, we talked about
Venice and about life and she was full of hope for me. Then I
told her about the voices and about the cook's hands on my
throat.

'You're imagining it, Henri, hold on to yourself, you'll be free
soon. There are no voices, no shapes.'

But there are. Under that stone, on the windowsill. There
are voices and they must be heard.

When Henri was taken to San Servelo in the grim boat I set
about procuring his release straight away. I tried to find out on
what grounds the insane are kept there and if they are ever
examined by a doctor to see if there has been any improvement.
It seems that they are, but only those who are no danger
to mankind can be let free. Absurd, when there are so
many dangers to mankind walking free without examination.
Henri was an inmate for life. There were no legal means of having him freed, at least not while Piero had anything to do with
it.

Well then, I would have to help him escape and ensure his passage to France.

For the first few months that I visited him he seemed cheerful and sanguine, despite sleeping in a room with three other men of hideous appearance and terrifying habits. He said he didn't notice them. He said he had his notebooks and he was busy. Perhaps there were signs of his change much earlier than I recognised, but my life had taken an unexpected turn and I was preoccupied.

I don't know what madness drove me to take a house opposite hers. A house with six storeys like hers, with long windows that let in the light and caught the sun in pools. I paced the floors of my house, never bothering to furnish any of them, looking in her sitting-room, her drawing-room, her sewing-room and seeing not her but a tapestry of myself when I was younger and walked like an arrogant boy.

I was beating a rug on my balcony when I finally saw her.

She saw me too and we stood like statues, each on our balconies. I dropped the rug into the canal.

'You are my neighbour,' she said. 'You should pay me a call,' and so it was fixed that I should pay her a call that evening before supper.

More than eight years had passed, but when I knocked on her door I didn't feel like an heiress who had walked from Moscow and seen her husband murdered. I felt like a Casino girl in a borrowed uniform. Instinctively, I put my hand to my heart. 'You've grown up,' she said.

She was the same, though she had let the grey show in her hair, something she had been particularly vain about when I knew her. We ate at the oval table and she seated us side by side again with the bottle in between. It wasn't easy to talk. It never had been, we were either too busy making love or afraid of being overheard. Why did I imagine things would be different simply because time had passed?

Where was her husband this evening?

He had left her.

Not for another woman. He didn't notice other women. He had left her quite recently to go on a voyage to find the Holy Grail. He believed his map to be definitive. He believed the treasure to be absolute.

'Will he come back?'

'He may, he may not.'

The wild card. The unpredictable wild card that never comes when it should. Had it fallen earlier; years earlier, what would have happened to me? I looked at my palms trying to see the other life, the parallel life. The point at which my selves broke away and one married a fat man and the other stayed here, in this elegant house to eat dinner night after night from an oval table.

Is this the explanation then when we meet someone we do not know and feel straight away that we have always known them? That their habits will not be a surprise. Perhaps our lives spread out around us like a fan and we can only know one life, but by mistake sense others.

When I met her I felt she was my destiny and that feeling has not altered, even though it remains invisible. Though I have taken myself to the wastes of the world and loved again, I cannot truly say that I ever left her. Sometimes, drinking coffee with friends or walking alone by the too salt sea, I have caught myself in that other life, touched it, seen it to be as real as my own. And if she had lived alone in that elegant house when I first met her? Perhaps I would never have sensed other lives of mine, having no need of them.

'Will you stay?' she said.

No, not in this life. Not now. Passion will not be commanded. It is no genie to grant us three wishes when we let it loose. It commands us and very rarely in the way we would choose.

I was angry. Whoever it is you fall in love with for the first time, not just love but be in love with, is the one who will always make you angry, the one you can't be logical about. It may be that you are settled in another place, it may be that you are happy, but the one who took your heart wields final power.

I was angry because she had wanted me and made me want her and been afraid to accept what that meant; it meant more than brief meetings in public places and nights borrowed from someone else. Passion will work in the fields for seven years for the beloved and on being cheated work for seven more, but passion, because it is noble, will not long accept another's left-overs.

I have had affairs. I will have more, but passion is for the single-minded.

She said again, 'Will you stay?'

When passion comes late in life for the first time, it is harder to give up. And those who meet this beast late in life are offered only devilish choices. Will they say goodbye to what they know and set sail on an unknown sea with no certainty of land again? Will they dismiss those everyday things that have made life tolerable and put aside the feelings of old friends, a lover even? In short, will they behave as if they are twenty years younger with Canaan just over the ridge?

Not usually.

And if they do, you will have to strap them to the mast as the boat pulls away because the siren calls are terrible to hear and they may go mad at the thought of what they have lost.

That is one choice.

Another is to learn to juggle; to do as we did for nine nights. This soon tires the hands if not the heart.

Two choices.

The third is to refuse the passion as one might sensibly refuse a leopard in the house, however tame it might seem at first. You might reason that you can easily feed a leopard and that your garden is big enough, but you will know in your dreams at least that no leopard is ever satisfied with what it's given. After nine nights must come ten and every desperate meeting only leaves you desperate for another. There is never enough to eat, never enough garden for your love.

So you refuse and then you discover that your house is haunted by the ghost of a leopard.

When passion comes late in life it is hard to bear.

One more night. How tempting. How innocent. I could stay tonight surely? What difference could it make, one more night? No. If I smell her skin, find the mute curves of her nakedness, she will reach in her hand and withdraw my heart like a bird's egg. I have not had time to cover my heart in barnacles to elude her. If I give in to this passion, my real life, the most solid, the best known, will disappear and I will feed on shadows again like those sad spirits whom Orpheus fled.

I wished her goodnight, touching her hand only and thankful for the dark that hid her eyes. I did not sleep that night, but wandered the unlit alleys, taking my comfort from the cool of the walls and the regular smack of the water. In the morning I shut up my house and never went there again.

And what of Henri?

As I told you, for the first few months, I thought him his old self. He asked for writing materials and seemed intent on re-creating his years since he had left home and his time with me. He loves me, I know that, and I love him, but in a brotherly incestuous way. He touches my heart, but he does not send it shattering through my body. He could never steal it. I wonder if things would be different for him if I could return his passion. No one ever has and his heart is too wide for his skinny chest. Someone should take that heart and give him peace. He used to say he loved Bonaparte and I believe him. Bonaparte, larger than life, sweeping him off to Paris, spreading his hand at the Channel and making Henri and those simple soldiers feel as if England belonged to them.

I have heard that when a duckling opens its eyes it will attach itself to whatever it first sees, duck or not. So it is with Henri, he opened his eyes and there was Bonaparte.

That's why he hates him so much. He disappointed him. Passion does not take disappointment well.

What is more humiliating than finding the object of your love unworthy?

Henri is a gentle man and I wonder if it was killing that fat cook that hurt his mind? He told me, on the way home from Moscow, that he had been in the army eight years without so much as wounding another man. Eight years of battle and the worst he'd done was to kill more chickens than he could count.

He was no coward though, he'd risked his own life over and over again to get a man off the field. Patrick told me that.

Henri.

I don't visit him now, but I wave from my boat every day at about this time.

When he said he was hearing voices – his mother's, the cook's, Patrick's – I tried to make him understand that there are no voices, only ones of our own making. I know the dead cry out sometimes, but I know too that the dead are greedy for attention and I urged him to shut them out and concentrate on himself. In a madhouse you must hold on to your mind.

He stopped telling me about them, but I heard from the warders that he woke up screaming night after night, his hands round his throat, sometimes nearly choked from self-strangling. This disturbed his fellows and they had him moved to a room by himself. He was much quieter after that, using the writing materials and a lamp I brought him. At that time I was still working for his release and confident of securing it. I was getting to know the warders and I had an idea that I could buy him out for money and sex. My red hair is a great attraction. I was still sleeping with him in those days. He had a thin boy's body that covered mine as light as a sheet and, because I had taught him to love me, he loved me well. He had no notion of what men do, he had no notion of what his own body did until I showed him. He gave me pleasure, but when I watched his face I knew it was more than that for him. If it disturbed me I put it aside. I have learnt to take pleasure without always questioning the source.

Two things happened.

I told him I was pregnant.

I told him he would be free in about a month.

'Then we can get married.'

'No.'

I took his hands and tried to explain that I wouldn't marry again and that he couldn't live in Venice and I wouldn't live in France.

'What about the child? How will I know about the child?'

'I'll bring the child when it's safe and you'll come here again when it's safe. I'll have Piero poisoned, I don't know, we'll find a way. You have to go home.'

He was silent and when we made love he put his hands to my throat and slowly pushed his tongue out of his mouth like a pink worm.

'I'm your husband,' he said.

'Stop it, Henri.'

'I'm your husband,' and he came leaning towards me, his eyes round and glassy and his tongue so pink.

I pushed him off and he curled in the corner and began to weep.

He wouldn't let me comfort him and we never made love again.

Not my doing.

The day came for his escape. I went to fetch him, running up the stairs two at a time, opening his door with my own key as I always did.

'Henri, you're a free man, come on.'

He stared at me.

'Patrick was here just now. You missed him.'

'Henri, come on.' I pulled him to his feet and shook his shoulders. 'We're leaving, look out of the window, there's our boat. It's a pageant boat, I got that sly Bishop again.'

'It's a long way down,' he said.

'You don't have to jump.'

'Don't I?'

His eyes were troubled. 'Can we get down the stairs in time? Will he catch us up?'

'There's no one to catch us. I've bribed them, we're on our way out and you'll never see this place again.'

'This is my home, I can't leave. What will mother say?'

I dropped my hands from his shoulders and put my hand under his chin.

'Henri. We're leaving. Come with me.'

He wouldn't.

Not that hour, nor the next, nor the next day and when the boat sailed I sailed it alone. He didn't come to the window.

'Go back to him,' said my mother. 'He'll be different next time.'

I went back to him, or rather I went to San Servelo. A polite warder from the respectable wing took tea with me and told me as nicely as he could that Henri didn't want to see me any more. Had expressly refused to see me.

'What's happened to him?'

The warder shrugged, a Venetian way of saying everything and nothing.

I went back dozens of times, always finding that he didn't

want to see me, always taking tea with the polite warder who wanted to be my lover and isn't.

A long time later, when I was rowing the lagoon and drifting out to his lonely rock, I saw him leaning from the window and I waved and he waved back and I thought then he might see me. He would not. Not me nor the baby, who is a girl with a mass of hair like the early sun and feet like his.

I row out every day now and he waves, but from my letters that are returned I know I have lost him.

Perhaps he has lost himself.

For myself, I still bask in church in the winter and on the warm walls in summer and my daughter is clever and already loves to see the dice fall and to spread the cards. I cannot save her from the Queen of spades nor any other, she will draw her lot when the time comes and gamble her heart away. How else could it be with such consuming hair? I am living alone. I prefer it that way, though I am not alone every night and increasingly I go to the Casino, to see old friends and to look at the case on the wall with two white hands.

The valuable, fabulous thing.

I don't dress up any more. No borrowed uniforms. Only occasionally do I feel the touch of that other life, the one in the shadows where I do not choose to live.

This is the city of disguises. What you are one day will not constrain you on the next. You may explore yourself freely and, if you have wit or wealth, no one will stand in your way. This city was built on wit and wealth and we have a fondness for both, though they do not have to appear in tandem.

I take my boat out on the lagoon and listen to the seagulls cry and wonder where I will be in eight years, say. In the soft darkness that hides the future from the over-curious, I content myself with this; that where I will be will not be where I am. The cities of the interior are vast, do not lie on any map.

And the valuable, fabulous thing?

Now that I have it back? Now that I have been given a reprieve such as only the stories offer?

Will I gamble it again?

Yes.

Après moi, le deluge.

Not really. A few drowned but a few have drowned before.

He over-estimated himself.

Odd that a man should come to believe in myths of his own making.

On this rock, the events in France hardly touched me. What difference could it make to me, safe at home with mother and my friends?

I was glad when they sent him to Elba. A quick death would have made him a hero straight away. Much better for reports to seep through of his increasing weight and bad temper. They were clever, those Russians and English, they did not bother to hurt him, they simply diminished him.

Now that he's dead, he's becoming a hero again and nobody minds because he can't make the most of it.

I'm tired of hearing his life-story over and over. He walks in here, small as it is, unannounced and takes up all my room. The only time I'm pleased to see him is when the cook's here, the cook's terrified of him and leaves at once.

They all leave their smells behind; Bonaparte's is chicken.

I keep getting letters from Villanelle. I send them back to her unopened and I never reply. Not because I don't think about her, not because I don't look for her from my window every day. I have to send her away because she hurts me too much.

There was a time, some years ago I think, when she tried to make me leave this place, though not to be with her. She was asking me to be alone again, just when I felt safe. I don't ever want to be alone again and I don't want to see any more of the world.

✳ The cities of the interior are vast and do not lie on any map.

The day she came was the day Domino died and I have not seen him. He doesn't come here.

I woke that morning and counted my possessions as I do; the Madonna, my notebooks, this story, my lamp and wicks, my pens and my talisman.

My talisman had melted. Only the gold chain remained, lying thin in a pool of water, glittering.

I picked it up and wrapped it around my fingers, strung it from one finger to another and watched how it slid like a snake. I knew then he was dead, though I do not know how or where. I put the chain around my neck, sure that she would notice it when she came but she didn't. Her eyes were bright and her hands were full of running away. I had run away with her before, come as an exile to her home and stayed for love. Fools stay for love. I am a fool. I stayed in the army eight years because I loved someone. You'd think that would have been enough. I stayed too because I had nowhere else to go.

I stay here by choice.

That means a lot to me.

She seemed to think we could reach her boat without being caught. Was she mad? I'd have to kill again. I couldn't do that, not even for her.

She told me she was going to have a baby but she didn't want to marry me.

How can that be?

I want to marry her and I'm not having her child.

It's easier not to see her. I don't always wave to her, I have a mirror and I stand slightly to one side of the window when she passes and if the sun is shining I can catch the reflection of her hair. It lights up the straw on the floor and I think the holy stable must have looked this way, glorious and humble and unlikely.

There's a child in the boat with her sometimes, it must be our daughter. I wonder what her feet are like.

Apart from my old friends, I don't talk to the people here. Not because they're mad and I'm not but because they lose concentration so quickly. It's hard to keep them on the same subject and, even if I do, it's not often a subject I'm much interested in.

What am I interested in?

Passion. Obsession.

I have known both and I know the dividing line is as thin and cruel as a Venetian knife.

When we walked from Moscow through the zero winter I believed I was walking to a better place. I believed I was taking action and leaving behind the sad and sordid things that had so long oppressed me. Free will, my friend the priest said, belongs to us all. The will to change. I don't take much account of scrying or sortilege. I'm not like Villanelle, I don't see hidden worlds in the palm of my hand nor a future in a clouded ball. And yet, what should I make of a gipsy who caught me in Austria and made the sign of the cross at my forehead saying, 'Sorrow in what you do and a lonely place.'

There has been sorrow in what I have done and if it were not for my mother and my friends here, this would be the most desolate spot.

At my window the seagulls cry. I used to envy them their freedom, them and the fields that stretched measuring distance, distance into distance. Every natural thing comfortable in its place. I thought a soldier's uniform would make me free because soldiers are welcome and respected and they know what will happen from one day to the next and uncertainty need not torment them. I thought I was doing a service to the world, setting it free, setting myself free in the process. Years passed,

I travelled distances that peasants never even think about and I found the air much the same in every country.

One battlefield is very like another.

There's a lot of talk about freedom. It's like the Holy Grail, we grow up hearing about it, it exists, we're sure of that, and every person has his own idea of where.

My friend the priest, for all his worldliness, found his freedom in God, and Patrick found it in a jumbled mind where goblins kept him company. Domino said it was in the present, in the moment only that you could be free, rarely and unexpectedly.

Bonaparte taught us that freedom lay in our fighting arm, but in the legends of the Holy Grail no one won it by force. It was Perceval, the gentle knight, who came to a ruined chapel and found what the others had overlooked, simply by sitting still. I think now that being free is not being powerful or rich or well regarded or without obligations but being able to love. To love someone else enough to forget about yourself even for one moment is to be free. The mystics and the churchmen talk about throwing off this body and its desires, being no longer a slave to the flesh. They don't say that through the flesh we are set free. That our desire for another will lift us out of ourselves more cleanly than anything divine.

We are a lukewarm people and our longing for freedom is our longing for love. If we had the courage to love we would not so value these acts of war.

At my window the seagulls cry. I should feed them, I save my breakfast bread so that I have something to give them.

Love, they say, enslaves and passion is a demon and many have been lost for love. I know this is true, but I know too that without love we grope the tunnels of our lives and never see the sun. When I fell in love it was as though I looked into a mirror for the first time and saw myself. I lifted my hand in wonderment and felt my cheeks, my neck. This was me. And when I had looked at myself and grown accustomed to who I was, I was not afraid to hate parts of me because I wanted to be worthy of the mirror bearer.

Then, when I had regarded myself for the first time, I regarded the world and saw it to be more various and beautiful than I thought. Like most people I enjoyed the hot evenings and the smell of food and the birds that spike the sky, but I was not a mystic nor a man of God and I did not feel the extasy I had read about. I longed for feeling though I could not have told you that. Words like passion and extasy, we learn them but they stay flat on the page. Sometimes we try and turn them over, find out what's on the other side, and everyone has a story to tell of a woman or a brothel or an opium night or a war. We fear it. We fear passion and laugh at too much love and those who love too much.

And still we long to feel.

I have started work on the garden here. No one has touched it for years, though I am told it once had fine roses of such a scent that you could smell them from St Mark's when the wind was right. Now it's a barbed tangle of thorns. Now the birds do not nest here. It's an inhospitable place and the salt makes it difficult to choose what to grow.

I dream of dandelions.

I dream of a wide field where flowers grow of their own accord. Today I shovelled away the soil from around the rockery, then shovelled it back, levelling the ground. Why have a rockery on a rock? We see enough rock.

I will write to Villanelle and ask for some seeds.

Strange to think that if Bonaparte hadn't divorced Joséphine, the geranium might never have come to France. She would have been too busy with him to develop her undoubted talent for botany. They say she has already brought us over a hundred different kinds of plants and that if you ask her she will send you seeds for nothing.

I will write to Joséphine and ask for some seeds.

My mother dried poppies in our roof and at Christmas made scenes from the Bible with the flower heads. I'm doing this garden partly for her; she says it's so barren here with nothing but the sea.

I'll plant some grass for Patrick and I want a headstone for Domino, nothing the others will find, just a stone in a warm place after all that cold.

And for myself?

For myself I will plant a cypress tree and it will outlive me. That's what I miss about the fields, the sense of the future as well as the present. That one day what you plant will spring up unexpectedly; a shoot, a tree, just when you were looking the other way, thinking about something else. I like to know that life will outlive me, that's a happiness Bonaparte never understood.

There's a bird here, a tiny bird that has no mother. I'm taking her place and the bird sits on my neck, behind my ear, keeping warm. I feed it milk and worms I dig up on my hands and knees, and yesterday it flew for the first time. Flew from the ground where I was planting and up to a thorn. It sang and I held out my finger to bring it home. At night it sleeps in my room in a collar box. I won't give it a name. I'm not Adam.

This is not a barren place. Villanelle, whose talent it is to look at everything at least twice, taught me to find joy in the most unlikely places and still to be surprised by the obvious. She had a knack of raising your spirits just by saying, 'Look at that,' and that was always an ordinary treasure brought to life. She can even charm the fishwives.

So I go from my room in the morning and make the journey to the garden very slowly, feeling the walls with my hands, getting a sense of surface, of texture. I breathe carefully, smelling the air, and when the sun is up I turn my face that way and let it lighten me.

I danced in the rain without my clothes one night. I had not done that before, not felt the icy drops like arrows and the change the skin undergoes. I've been soaked through in the army times without number but not by choice.

In the rain by choice is a different matter, though the warders didn't think so. They threatened to take my bird away.

At the garden, although I have a spade and a fork, I often dig with my hands if it's not too cold. I like to feel the earth, to squeeze it hard and tight or to crumble it between my fingers.

There's time here to love slowly.

The man who walks on water has asked me to include a pond in my garden so that he can practise.

He's an Englishman. What do you expect?

There's a warder who's fond of me. I don't ask why, I've learnt to take what's there without questioning the source. When he sees me on all fours scrabbling at the earth in a random-looking way that is quite scientific, he gets upset and hurries over with the spade and offers to help me. Especially, he wants me to use the spade.

He doesn't understand I want the freedom to make my own mistakes.

'You'll never get out, Henri, not if they think you're mad.' Why would I want to get out? They're so preoccupied with getting out they miss what's here. When the day warders go off in their boats I don't stand and stare. I wonder where they go and what their lives are like, but I wouldn't change places with them. Their faces are grey and unhappy even on the sunniest days when the wind whips at the rock for its own delight.

Where would I go? I have a room, a garden, company and time for myself. Aren't these the things people ask for?

And love?

I am still in love with her. Not a day breaks but that I think of her, and when the dogwood turns red in winter I stretch out my hands and imagine her hair.

I am in love with her; not a fantasy or a myth or a creature of my own making.

Her. A person who is not me. I invented Bonaparte as much as he invented himself.

My passion for her, even though she could never return it, showed me the difference between inventing a lover and falling in love.

The one is about you, the other about someone else.

I have had a letter from Joséphine. She remembers me and she wants to visit me here, though I expect that's impossible. She showed no alarm at the address and has enclosed seeds of many kinds, some to be grown under glass. I have instructions and in some cases illustrations, though what I am to do with a baobab tree I don't know. Apparently it grows upside down.

Perhaps this is the best place for it.

They say that when Joséphine was in the slimy prison of Carmes waiting for death at the hands of the Terror, she and other ladies of strong character cultivated the weeds and lichens that spread in the stone and managed to make for themselves, while not a garden, a green place that comforted them. It may or may not be true.

It doesn't matter.

Hearing about it comforts me.

Over the water in that city of madmen they are preparing for Christmas and New Year. They don't make much of Christmas apart from the Child, but they have a procession at New Year and the decorated boats are easy to see from my window. Their lights bob up and down and the water beneath shines like oil. I stay up the whole night, listening to the dead moan round the rock and watching the stars move across the sky.

At midnight the bells ring out from every one of their churches and they have a hundred and seven at least. I have tried to count, but it is a living city and no one really knows what buildings are there from one day to the next.

You don't believe me?
Go and see for yourself.

We have a service here on San Servelo and a ghoulish business
it is with most of the inmates in chains and the rest jabbering
or fidgeting so much that for the few who care it's impossible
to hear the Mass. I don't go now, it's not a place to bask. I prefer
to stay in my room and look out of the window. Last year
Villanelle came by in her boat, as close as she could get, and let
off fireworks. One exploded so high that I almost touched it and
for a second I thought I might drop down after those falling rays
and touch her too, once more. Once more, what difference
could it make to be near her again? Only this. That if I start to
cry I will never stop.

I re-read my notebook today and I found:

I say I'm in love with her, what does that mean?
It means I review my future and my past in the light of this
feeling. It is as though I wrote in a foreign language that I am
suddenly able to read. Wordlessly she explains me to myself;
like genius she is ignorant of what she does.

I go on writing so that I will always have something to read.

There is a frost tonight that will brighten the ground and harden
the stars. In the morning when I go into the garden I'll find it
webbed with nets of ice and cracked ice where I over-watered
today. Only the garden freezes like that, the rest is too salty.

I can see the lights on the boats and Patrick, who is with me,
can see into St Mark's itself. His eye is still marvellous, especially
so since walls no longer get in the way. He describes to me the
altar boys in red and the Bishop in his crimson and gold and on
the roof the perpetual battle between good and evil. The painted
roof that I love.

It's more than twenty years since we went to church at Boulogne.

Out now, into the lagoon, the boats with their gilded prows and triumphant lights. A bright ribbon, a talisman for the New Year.

I will have red roses next year. A forest of red roses.

On this rock? In this climate?

I'm telling you stories. Trust me.

ABOUT THE AUTHOR

Born in Lancashire in 1959, Jeanette Winterson was raised by a family of Pentecostal evangelists and destined to be a missionary. When this didn't work out, she left home for several odd jobs before studying English at Oxford. She then worked in the theater and lived a life of poverty until writing her first novel, *Oranges Are Not the Only Fruit.* She lives in London's Gospel Oak, where she practices karate and drives a very old sports car. Recipient of the Whitbread Prize for best first novel and the John Llewellyn Rhys Prize for best writer under thirty-five, Winterson is currently at work on a new book.

THE STRANGER
by Albert Camus

Through the story of an ordinary man who unwittingly gets drawn into a senseless murder, Camus explores what he termed "the nakedness of man faced with the absurd."

0-679-72020-0/$7.95

....

THE REMAINS OF THE DAY
by Kazuo Ishiguro

A profoundly compelling portrait of the perfect English butler and of his fading, insular world in postwar England.

"One of the best books of the year."

—*The New York Times Book Review*

0-679-73172-5/$9.95

....

THE WOMAN WARRIOR
by Maxine Hong Kingston

"A remarkable book...As an account of growing up female and Chinese-American in California, in a laundry of course, it is anti-nostalgic; it burns the fat right out of the mind. As a dream—of the 'female avenger'—it is dizzying, elemental, a poem turned into a sword."

—*The New York Times*

0-679-72188-6/$9.00

....

MY TRAITOR'S HEART
by Rian Malan

Rian Malan, a former crime reporter who fled his country after witnessing unimaginable atrocities, returns in search of the truth behind apartheid.

"Here is truth-telling at its most exemplary and courageous. The remorseless exercise of a reporter's anguished conscience gives us a South Africa we thought we knew all about: but we knew nothing."

—John le Carré

0-679-73215-2/$10.95

....

DEATH IN VENICE AND SEVEN OTHER STORIES
by Thomas Mann

In addition to *Death in Venice* ("A story," Mann said, "of death...of the voluptuousness of doom"), this volume includes "Mario the Magician," "Disorder and Early Sorrow," "A Man and His Dog," "Felix Krull," "The Blood of the Walsungs," "Tristan," and "Tonio Kröger."

0-679-72206-8/$8.95

. . . .

LOLITA
by Vladimir Nabokov

The controversial novel that tells the story of the aging Humbert Humbert's obsessive, devouring, and doomed passion for the nymphet Dolores Haze.

"The only convincing love story of our century."
—*Vanity Fair*

0-679-72316-1/$8.95

. . . .

NO EXIT AND THREE OTHER PLAYS
by Jean-Paul Sartre

No Exit is an unforgettable portrayal of hell. *The Flies* is a modern reworking of the Electra-Orestes story. *Dirty Hands* is about a young intellectual torn between theory and praxis. *The Respectful Prostitute* is a scathing attack on American racism.

0-679-72516-4/$9.00

. . . .

THE PASSION
by Jeanette Winterson

Intertwining the destinies of two remarkable people—the soldier Henri, for eight years Napoleon's faithful cook, and Villanelle, the red-haired daughter of a Venetian boatman—*The Passion* is "a deeply imagined and beautiful book, often arrestingly so" *(The New York Times Book Review)*.

0-679-72437-0/$9.00

. . . .